D1582838

C

MARK GERSON

)UT THE AUTHOR

Creasey is the most prolific writer
ır age. Since the publication of his
mystery in 1931, this English writer
written roughly 35 million words.
:otal output of books is close to the
mark with all editions coming to
ıver 2,000.

THE SCENE
OF THE CRIME

By

John Creasey

CHARLES SCRIBNER'S SONS

New York

THE SCENE
OF THE CRIME

1

THE FIRST CRIME

When Alice came towards him, eyes glowing, great eagerness and love in her, John Payne felt the first twinge of conscience, the first hint of shame. He crushed them. She had thrown herself at his head from the beginning, and but for her the crime would never have been planned. Curiously, for the first time he saw how attractive she was in her demure way; perhaps that was because she was touched with radiance and excitement. She was twenty-three, and looked younger. She had quite nice legs and arms, but hardly any figure; with her hair cut short, as she liked to wear it, and in trousers, she was more like a youth than a young woman. She walked well, and clutched her handbag tightly.

It was ludicrous for her to think that she might ever lure him away from Gwen. She knew Gwen slightly; and anyone who met his wife must be aware of her surging vitality, must surely know that there was hardly a woman who could hold a man against her. Yet he was sure that Alice had fooled herself. An occasional meal, a drink together, a few evenings in the back row of a suburban cinema, two evenings at her flatlet and—promises. She had needed nothing else to convince herself that he was in love with her.

Poor, simple Alice.

It was a clear winter evening, with the stars out, and the street lamplight shone to give her an added sparkle. Payne was standing in the doorway of a shop near the cinema, and she was looking out for him, but had not yet seen him. When he stepped forward, her eyes lit up.

She looked quite beautiful.

"Darling!" she breathed, in that whispering way she had

acquired because of the furtiveness of their meetings. "I've got it!"

"Wonderful," Payne breathed. "Wonderful!" He drew her into the shop doorway, and she came in eagerly. He slid his right arm round her and pressed her close to him, then sought her lips, and kissed her with a simulation of passion which had always deceived her. When he drew back, she was gasping a little and the light sparkled starlike in her eyes. "Alice," Payne whispered, "you're beautiful —even more beautiful tonight."

"You're the most handsome man in the world," she whispered back.

She meant it—as years ago, Gwen had meant it. Now his hair was greying a little, but he still dressed well; at forty-seven he had no stomach to speak of, could still play squash, racquets or tennis vigorously, and had the hard, chiselled look of the outdoor man.

"Did you have any trouble?" Payne asked.

"Not really." She was beginning to open her handbag already. She was never too demanding, was satisfied with surprisingly little. She took out a small, sealed package, about the size of a packet of twenty cigarettes, and handed it to him. "There it is."

She put it into his hand.

He took it, and held it very tightly, then took her hands with his free one, and squeezed, drawing her to him again. He could feel the feathery softness of her breath upon his cheeks, and the beating of her heart betraying the tumult within her.

"Wonderful," he said again, and slid the package into his pocket.

It was the key to Anderson's strongroom.

She believed that it was the key to their future, that with it he would steal enough money and jewels to take them out of England. She really believed that he would settle somewhere in Europe with her, perhaps even farther afield. Winning her round to face the actual theft had been the difficult, delicate task; it had taken many months, of hints, suggestions, words of love and longing.

If only they had sufficient money, nothing else would stop them. If only, if only, if only . . .

That hardly mattered now. She had been won round, after the first sharp reaction against it, and one by one she had brought him keys of the safes, taking them back after he had made replicas. She had never doubted that she would be able to get hold of the complicated strongroom key long enough for him to make a replica; or that she could get it back to Anderson's flat without the old man knowing that it had ever been missing. She had tried to take an impression of the key on soap and plasticine, but the rounded barrel and the intricate cutting had made it essential to work from the key itself.

She did not know that it was virtually a key to her coffin.

That was an ugly thought; Payne did not like it, and told himself that now the time was getting nearer he must not become soft-hearted. With her alive, the whole scheme would fall down, for he would be far too vulnerable. He must not even think of the possibility of leaving her alive.

"What do you mean—you didn't really have any trouble?" Payne made himself ask.

"Just as I was leaving his bedroom, his son came in," Alice answered. "I had to stay and be nice to him for nearly half an hour! The key was burning a hole in my—" She broke off, gave a little laugh which he knew indicated the tension she felt, and went on—"I'd dropped the key down the front of my dress, to make sure Julian—"

"I'd like to break his neck!" Payne exclaimed, and there was a harsh note of ferocity in his manner; that would please her. One thing she disliked more than any other was having to endure some of the little attentions of Julian Anderson.

Alice said: "Oh, I can handle Julian all right now!" She was looking up into Payne's face, and there was only one word for her expression: adoring. "I had to stay until he was ready to go, he was the only one who might possibly have noticed that the key was missing."

"Alice," said Payne, huskily, "you're absolutely superb. You've got nerves of steel."

"A year ago I would have been so scared I would have dropped the key in front of his eyes," Alice said. "Darling, I wonder if you know how good you've been for me! Until I knew you, I wasn't much more than a schoolgirl. Now—" She broke off, and laughed again. "When—when do you think you can do it, John?"

"I think about this time next month," he said. "The middle of February."

"I can hardly wait!"

"How do you think I feel?" Payne demanded. "I won't delay a minute longer than necessary. When it's over, we'll wait for a week or two, then go across to the Continent separately." He caught his breath. "*You* can hardly wait," he echoed roughly. "I wish to God we could spend the evening together, but I must get this duplicate made tonight. It would be tempting fate to keep the key any longer. What will you do while you're waiting?"

"I might as well go to the pictures," Alice said, philosophically. "There's quite a good main feature on." She gave that little, nervous laugh again. "A crime story!"

"Just right for the night," agreed Payne. "I'll be finished by eleven o'clock, so if you'll catch a Number 22 bus and get off at the usual place, we can snatch half an hour together."

"Wonderful," Alice said; and she meant it.

Payne took a slim box of chocolates from his topcoat pocket and gave it to her; she was as pleased as if it were a sumptuous box. He kissed her fiercely again, then let her go. Immediately, she turned her back on him and walked briskly towards the entrance to the cinema. A middle-aged man, passing, glanced at him; a policeman was coming along on the other side of the road. Payne stepped out of the shop doorway, took out cigarettes, lit one, and looked towards Alice. She was disappearing, and did not look round. She

had learned all the tricks of deception, of making sure that
they were not seen together too often, and that they did
nothing to attract attention. He had used Gwen as a bogey,
and often wondered how he would explain Alice away to
Gwen, if it should ever become necessary.

He did not think it would.

He went a hundred yards along Fulham Road, where his
small car was parked, a ten-year-old Austin. He got in, but
did not start the engine immediately; he needed a respite.
He slid his hand into his pocket and touched the key, then
suddenly laughed to himself. The laughter became almost un-
controllable; he had to stifle it, to make sure that he did not
startle passers-by. Reaction, of course. He had the key, he
already had the dummy ready, one of the right type and
size which it would be easy to cut. Even if he didn't finish
tonight, he could make an impression of this one, and finish
the job tomorrow.

The timing was perfect.

They had waited months for the opportunity, knowing
that it was bound to come, for every winter old Anderson
went down with his bronchitis, and was so afraid of com-
plications that he stayed indoors, mostly in his room, doing
only essential work. Alice was his secretary, and she went to
his room every morning and afternoon, to take down letters
and to take them back for signing. Payne wondered how she
had managed to get the key off the ring, but she had often
told him that the keys themselves were in a drawer of the
dressing-table in the room. He, Payne, had never been inside that room, but she had described it so well that he almost
believed he knew it, with the red, mahogany furniture, the
big mirrors, the huge dressing-table, the high bed, the easy
chair close to it, the small desk where Alice worked.

How she had contrived it didn't matter; the important
thing was that Anderson should never know that the key
had been out of his possession.

The next twenty-four hours would be the tricky ones.
Twenty-four hours, at the end of those long months of think-

ing, dreaming, planning. It was over a year since he had first thought about robbing Anderson's, where he had worked five years ago, but had left, so as to start his own business. He had been so full of confidence at the time, so sure of success, but he hadn't made a go of it.

The worst thing about that had been letting Gwen down.

The thought of robbing Anderson's had come when he had gone to try to sell the old man some French jewellery, and Anderson had taken him downstairs and shown him that the place was still in a hopeless confusion. That was the day he had first met Alice, too, and he had sensed how he impressed her. After that, it had been easy to meet her 'by chance', easy to cultivate her, although more difficult to win her round to what he wanted to do.

He was in a perfect position to dispose of the stolen goods, too, for his own business was that of buying up second-hand and antique jewellery, polishing it, sometimes resetting, and always reselling it. With a few thousand pounds in capital he could have made a fortune; and he had always promised Gwen a fortune. Now it was all over bar the shouting.

Payne started the engine and drove off; in twenty minutes he was in the garage of his Richmond home. Gwen and the youngsters were out, it was as if everything was conspiring to give him exactly the opportunity he wanted. He did not go into the house, but went straight to the workshop at the back of the garage, where he did his polishing and resetting. He had a few tools, a small lathe, a little stock of old gold and silver settings, everything he needed.

Except plenty of stock.

Once he got all he wanted from Anderson he would release the stock cautiously, over a period of years. It would be worth that fortune all right, and would get him and Gwen out of this rabbit-hutch into a decent house. He would show Gwen that he wasn't a big-mouthed braggart, too.

He kept the shutters up at the workshop, working in artificial light, so that neighbours shouldn't know that he

was there. Then he put on his raincoat, to keep his suit
clean, and set to work.

It should take an hour to make the key . . .

It took him exactly fifty-five minutes.

He had two keys then, absolutely identical, as well as the
master keys to the safes in the strongroom beneath the shop.
What an old fool Anderson was! He should have built in
new safes years ago—he, John Payne, had recommended
that he should when he had worked for the old miser, and
Anderson had always said:

"Yes, I must, I will. I'll get round to it, one day."

The mean old so-and-so.

Payne held the new key up to the light, turned it round
and round in his fingers, gloatingly, then put it in the false
bottom of his toolbox, with the others; keys to a fortune—
and keys to Alice's coffin. That ugly thought came again,
giving Payne a ghoulish feeling.

It passed.

He wiped his fingerprints off the original key, and
wrapped it up again. Then he went outside, switching off
the light of the garage. For the second time that night he
noticed a policeman, this time one near the front gate of
the small semi-detached house not far from the Upper Richmond Road.

The policeman said: "Good evening, sir."

"Evening," Payne returned, heartily. "Just going out,"
he added unnecessarily, and stepped to his car. "Nice night."

"Very cold though," the policeman said.

Cold, thought Payne, and felt one of those paroxysms of
laughter coming on; he had to fight to control it. When it
had passed, he drove off. It was too early for Alice, but he
had to be away before Gwen arrived. Gwen believed that
he was at the Sports Club playing billiards; there was always
a chance that one of the other members would ask her why
he hadn't shown up, but that was another risk he had to
take. He had always been able to concentrate on the immediate task, without worrying about what would come next.

Tonight he had the key.

Tomorrow he had to make sure that Alice could never tell anyone about that.

Tomorrow, or the next day—

"No," he said angrily. "Tomorrow."

As he drove slowly towards Putney, he kept seeing a picture of Alice in his mind's eye. Why had she seemed so attractive tonight? Why did she remind him so vividly of his own daughter? They weren't even remotely alike, for Hilda took after Gwen in every way. When his son Maurice felt in a teasing mood, he could make Hilda angry to a point of tears by making bland references to Sabrina or Jayne.

"My God!" Payne exclaimed. "Do I need a drink!"

He wasn't quite himself. Something was working inside him so that he was not as cold and calculating as he wanted to be. Ahead, the lights of a pub showed yellow, and brighter light streamed out as two men came from it. Payne slowed down. A double whisky was exactly what he needed to put him right. He pulled up opposite the pub, switched off the engine, sat still for a moment, and then said in the same rough angry voice:

"Don't be a bloody fool. I can have a drink when it's all over, if I start knocking whisky back now I'll have had it." He started the engine again, and drove off much faster than he intended. He would have to wait nearly an hour to see Alice again. It was almost a pity that he had to, tonight, but until the key was safely back with Anderson, this first part of the job wouldn't be finished.

*   *   *

He saw Alice step lightly off a bus, and stand for a moment looking up and down. His car was parked near the tow path, where there was little light. She came hurrying towards it.

At least she would die happy.

2

FAMILY

THE next evening, there was a drizzle of rain, making the
light shimmer on wet roads. Alice was a little late. Even
two or three minutes seemed a long time to Payne while he
stood in the doorway near another cinema, this time at
Hammersmith; they seldom met in the same place twice in
succession. Traffic swished by. A bell rang with urgent warning, and a white ambulance passed; Payne saw it swing off
towards Chiswick. He was clenching his teeth hard. They had
been due to meet at half past six, and now it was twenty-five
minutes to seven. Two buses passed, and he stared at the plat-
forms, hoping that Alice was on one of them, but she was not.

A police car went by very swiftly, carrying the same air
of urgency as the ambulance; and a big black Humber,
with four or five big men inside it, swung along behind the
police car. Payne had a feeling that they were from Scotland Yard, and blamed his edginess for the thought. He
watched the Humber as it swung round the corner towards
Chiswick, and the light of another car showed the men
inside clearly; big, hulking shapes.

"Hallo, darling," Alice said.

Payne swung round, and startled her because his expression was so tense.

"John, what—" She began.

He took her forearm and drew her into the shop doorway.
His heart was thumping, and he could see that he had
alarmed her. For a moment he could not get words out, and
she asked again, anxiously:

"John, what is it? Are you all right?"

"I—I thought something had happened to you," he managed to say.

15

"Of course it hasn't," replied Alice. "Everything went off perfectly. I—I had a little difficulty getting away from Julian again, that's all, he followed me to the bus stop!"

Payne said: "Oh. Oh, I see. I was afraid—" He broke off, found his voice more easily, and went on with a savage note: "I couldn't stand it if anything happened to you, don't you understand?"

"Yes," Alice said, very quietly. "I understand because it's exactly what I feel about you, darling. But I'm not very late."

"Hardly at all, really, but—" Payne broke off. "Oh, it doesn't matter. You're sure there was no trouble?"

"When I got to Mr. Anderson's room this morning, he was having a bath," Alice said. "I was able to put the key back on the chain with ten minutes to spare. Darling, I always knew how easy it would be!" She was a little choky with excitement. "But I wish—"

"What?"

"I wish my part weren't over," she said. "I wish I could help you when it comes to—to taking what we want."

Could anyone be more naïve?

"You don't want to be anywhere near when that happens," Payne said, firmly. "That's essential. You've got to have an alibi, and—anyhow, no one will ever suspect you."

They would, of course. When they discovered that the safes and strongroom had been opened by a duplicate master-key, she would be the first person to be questioned, and she would not be able to stand up to the police. That was another reason why it was essential that she should die; and why it should be over soon.

Tonight.

He was smiling, hiding his edginess.

"That's why we're waiting a few weeks before breaking in," he said. "The old man's bronchitis will have been forgotten by then."

"I hope so," Alice said, and startled him by laughing. Every now and again something unexpected amused her, and her laugh could be most attractive. "Oh, I'm not worried at all, darling. I trust you absolutely, and—it's rather funny really, isn't it?"

Funny!

"What is?"

"Everything," said Alice. "There was a time when the very thought of having anything to do with this would have horrified me, and now I wish that I could do more! I hope I don't become a hardened criminal."

"Keep your voice low," Payne said urgently, although there was no need to caution her, he simply needed a moment's respite. "We—we'll never have to do anything like this again. We'll get enough to last us for the rest of our lives, and—sweetheart, everything is going to be just as we planned."

"I've never doubted it," Alice said, and turned her face upwards, to his. He hadn't kissed her, he had been so worked up. He kissed her now, rather gently, the obvious reason being that this doorway was shallow, and more people could see them. He let her go.

"Must you go home now?" Alice asked. She wasn't really demanding more, just speaking wistfully.

"I hate it," Payne said, "but I mustn't risk my wife asking a lot of questions, must I?"

"No," Alice agreed. "She—" She hesitated for a moment, and then asked in a rather louder voice than usual: "Are you sure she'll give you the divorce?"

Payne said, very softly: "There isn't a shadow of doubt. I've told you that time and time again, but there mustn't be any upset just now. Until everything's over, I need to be as normal as possible. She mustn't have the slightest reason to suspect there's anything wrong."

"Of course not," Alice said. "I do understand, darling."

Payne said: "If I had my way, I would spend every minute of the night and day with you." He managed to speak as if with passionate feeling, and drew her to him, kissing her as if he could not hold back his desire. Then he stood her to one side, almost roughly. "I've got to go! I don't trust myself. I'll see you on Monday, at Sloane Square."

"Yes, darling."

"Three whole days," Payne said, as if he hated the thought. "Three—" He broke off, and then thrust his hand into his pocket and drew out the slim box of chocolates. "Alice, I really don't trust myself. I've got to leave you. See you Monday." He thrust the chocolates into her hand, squeezed her arms, and turned and strode off. For a few seconds, he could hardly see where he was going, he was so disturbed and distressed. For some ridiculous reason, he hated lying to her. If she hadn't told him how utterly she trusted him he would not have felt so badly, but here he was, planning her murder, knowing exactly how he was going to kill her that very night; and those clear, trusting, beautiful eyes seemed to damn him, and her whispering voice seemed to mock.

He did not look back.

He went home, arriving a little after seven o'clock—his normal time on a Friday. As he opened the front door, he heard the loud voice of someone on the television, and hesitated for a moment before closing the front door. Then he heard Maurice laughing. Hilda said something, and Payne gathered that they were in one of their really friendly moods; they often were, although Hilda was two years older, at eighteen, and Maurice sometimes showed a sixteen-year-old's crudeness and unthinking unkindness. They were wonderful kids. *Wonderful.* Payne took off his hat and coat as the door of the living-room opened, and Gwen appeared, outlined against the light.

"Hallo, darling," she greeted in her rather deep voice; the voice which was always on the point of breaking into laughter. "I thought I felt a draught!" She came along towards him, tall, big for a woman, with a magnificent figure. She had a swaying walk which she could do nothing about, and was inclined to wear her clothes too tightly, as

well as to have her neckline too daring; but that was Gwen.
She drew up. "All right, dear?"

"Yes," said Payne. "Yes, of course it is, why shouldn't
it be?" Quite suddenly, he felt afraid, and that put extra
vigour into the way he took her arms and held her to him;
extra feeling into his evening kiss. He wanted to stay alone
with her, did not want to go into the room with the children,
for she was a great source of strength. In the few seconds
which passed he told himself that he would alarm her or
give her reason to think there was something serious the
matter if he went on like this, so he let her go and said
heartily: "Whatever's cooking smells good."

He could hardly smell a thing.

"Forgotten that your wife is a good cook?" Gwen asked
lightly. So she had noticed nothing, and turned away from
him. He thrust his arms round her, and pressed her back
against him for a moment; that was normal, and that was
how he felt about her, too. She laughed, put her hands on
his for a moment and said:

"We don't want the children to see, they learn too fast as
it is."

"Children," he echoed, and let her go. "They'll be teaching us before long." He went along with her, suddenly happier, the tension gone, the fear lifted. Gwen opened the door
wide, and Maurice looked round from the television set, then
jumped up. That must have been quite an effort, for a
Western serial was on; his *grande passion.*

"Hallo, Dad!"

"Hallo, old chap. How's Deadshot Dick?"

"Doing fine," said Maurice. He was tall for his age,
rather thin, almost an ugly duckling, but he had a twinkle
in his eyes.

Hilda was putting down some frilly things she had been
mending. She was a natural blonde, with a fair skin which
had hardly a blemish, quite beautiful blue eyes, and those
incredibly vital statistics; when they were forgotten she was
the most natural girl in the world.

"Hallo, Dad!"

"Hi, Topsy," said Payne, and kissed her lightly, but on the instant he seemed to see Alice in her place. He waited until the moment passed; it did not last long. He clapped his hands together heartily, and went on: "First food and then slippers and the fireside with my dutiful family," he boomed. He was overdoing the heartiness, but could not prevent himself. Gwen, her hair still flaxen, was going into the kitchen, and Hilda began to lay the table.

"You didn't forget the chocolates, Dad, did you?" she asked.

"On a Friday? Certainly not," said Payne. Again he felt a twinge as of compunction, but it soon passed. "They're on the hallstand." He went out to get a pound box, every Friday night's treat for fifteen years. He was glad of a few moments' respite, and when he went back the table was laid and a sizzling sausage toad was in front of his place. "My!" he exclaimed, "that's about the record, isn't it?"

His appetite was nearly as good as Maurice's, and Gwen did not yet need to check hers.

Payne brought the chocolates out about a quarter to ten, and wondered how many Alice had eaten from her smaller box. He was quite composed, and the tendency to be too loud had gone; he was in complete control of himself, as he believed he would be until it was all over.

He selected his own chocolates carefully, as he always had; it was a family joke that he should have first choice. He chose those without even a slight blemish on the top, for the blemish marked the ones which contained a sleeping draught. It had been quite a job, getting the capsules, taking out the contents, making it into a paste, inserting it in the chocolates with an icing syringe. Only if someone examined the chocolates carefully could anyone find out that they had been tampered with.

He wanted the family to sleep soundly tonight, while he was out.

Just as Alice, whose chocolates had been treated in exactly

the same way, would sleep soundly—with the gas hissing from the fire in her room. He had once thought of poisoning Alice with chocolates, but although sleeping powder was fairly easy to come by, deadly poison was difficult, and might be traced back to him.

At half past ten, Gwen said: "I don't know what's the matter with me, I must have eaten too much. I think I'll go up early, Jack." There was the inevitable glint of laughter in her eyes. "*You* may stay down and read."

"I'll see about that," he said, ominously.

Hilda was already upstairs, getting ready for bed, and Maurice would be in bed within a few minutes.

Alice . . . ?

Payne went upstairs at half past eleven, and found all the family sound asleep. He crept downstairs, let himself out the back way, walked stealthily to the garage and took out Maurice's bicycle. He wheeled this into the street when he was sure that no one was about, and cycled towards Alice's rooms in Chelsea. He wore thin cotton gloves, and his hands were very cold when he reached the corner of Manville Street. Two men were walking briskly along on the other side of the road. They did not appear to take any notice of him. He heard a little gasp of sound, looked round, and saw a couple in a doorway. He wheeled the bicycle into a car park where several cars were standing, put the chain round the back wheel and locked it, then walked briskly towards the next corner. Just round it, Alice had a bed-sitting-room and kitchenette in a house which had been converted into a dozen small flats. The street door was always locked about midnight, but not bolted, and he had a key. He stepped inside, closed the door very softly, and stood listening. The sound of music came faintly, probably from a record-player. He went up the linoleum-covered stairs towards Alice's room on the third floor. The music was coming from a room near hers, and helped to cover any sound he made.

He opened Alice's door with a key, just a crack at first; there was only darkness beyond. His heart began to thump.

He stepped inside softly, and the music sounded farther away. He closed the door hesitatingly, in case it made too much of a click; he hardly heard it close. He stood with his back to it, looking across at the divan bed against the door wall. He could just make out the white sheet, and Alice's dark head on the pillow. The music was a long way off and he believed that he could hear Alice breathing. He stepped towards the fireplace. The room was familiar, although he had seldom been here; whenever he had, he had made sure that he studied the layout of the room, and the position of the furniture.

There was an armchair by the fire, a small table next to it, and a box on the table. Used to the light, now, Payne saw that the box was open, and three parts empty. That labour had not been in vain! He felt in his pocket for his matches, and then thought: *Fool!* He wasn't going to *light* the gas. He picked up the box of chocolates and put it into his pocket; the paper inside rustled loudly. He glanced round, and made sure that Alice hadn't stirred. How could she? She would probably sleep until ten o'clock next morning.

He winced, realising that his mind had almost rejected what he was going to do. She would sleep if left alone, but when the gas filled the room she would pass out of sleep into death.

He bent down, and turned on the tap; there was a faint hiss, followed immediately by a smell of gas. He turned the tap on fuller.

The fire was only two yards from the bed.

He went across to the window, and began to push the top half up cautiously, closing it tightly; then he drew the curtains. He looked across the room, to make sure that the door leading to the little kitchen was closed. The main door fitted flush, and he had noticed how difficult it was to push open when he had first come in here; everything had worked out perfectly, as if this had been willed to happen without hindrance. The police might suspect murder, but there was no way they could prove it, certainly none in which they could trace it to him.

The gas hissed; that and his breathing were the only sounds he could hear. He stood by the foot of the bed, looking down on Alice, and for the first time since he had entered he felt frightened. He gritted his teeth, moved swiftly, and stepped to the door. His hand was actually on the handle when he heard the movement at the bed, and as he turned his head, he saw the light go on.

Alice's arms was stretched out towards it, and Alice was hitching herself up in bed, staring at him.

3

THE MURDER

PAYNE saw her vividly, and knew that she had recognised him. She had that long, thin arm stretched out, still touching the lamp switch. Her eyes looked huge. Her lips were parted, as if she were about to scream for help; but when she realised who it was, they moved, and formed his name: "*John.*"

She must have been awake a long time; time enough to see him moving about the room, and to realise what he was doing.

"I—I just had to see you," he said jerkily. "I just couldn't keep away." He could not tell whether she would believe him, but had to keep her quiet until he was near enough to—to strangle her. He knew that was the only thing to do.

He saw the puzzlement in her eyes as he drew nearer, and something in his expression must have warned her. Terror flared up in her, and she snatched her hand from the switch to strike at him. Then the room seemed to go round and round, and there were hard, confused noises; she had knocked the lamp off the bedside table. She brought her clenched fist down on the side of his head, but it made no difference to him, and at last his fingers closed about her slender throat. The lamp crashed. Strange shadows filled the room. Light and shade were upon her face, making her look like a gargoyle, as hideous as he must be. The only things he could see clearly were her enormous eyes, bright with terror, eyes close to him, eyes which began to close. He saw her lips twisting, writhing. He felt her beating at him, his head, his shoulders. He felt his fingers burying themselves in her flesh, and he squeezed and squeezed.

Her eyes closed; it was as if a light had gone out.

He kept squeezing, although his right shoulder was pressed awkwardly against the head of the bed; his left hand was quite free.

He was sure that she had stopped breathing, but dared not take the slightest chance of being wrong. Now there was another fear, that someone below or next door had heard the lamp fall, and would come to find out if Alice was all right. He crouched there, sprawled across the bed, fingers still embedded in the soft throat, head turned so that he could see the door, gasping for breath and yet trying to keep silent, to be sure that no one was coming.

All he could hear was a thudding in his own ears and his chest.

He stared more fixedly at the door, the handle especially; it did not turn. He began to ease his position so that he could move more freely, but did not look away from the door. He must have been there for three or four minutes before he began to take his hands away, and the fingers seemed as if they were held tight by the flesh; he had to pluck them away.

He shivered, violently.

He straightened up, pushed his gloved hands through his hair, and then thought in panic : *I mustn't leave any hairs in here!* He snatched his hands down, and stood staring at Alice. She did not look very different, really, there was only puffiness at her neck, a kind of relaxed look on her face. He moved convulsively, snatched at the sheet and pulled it up over her head.

He shivered again.

The light was so strange, the shadows so peculiar. Of course; that lamp was on the floor. He hesitated, then stepped to the door, switched on the main light, and looked round the room. He was glad that he had covered Alice's face. As far as he could see, little had been disturbed, after all. He righted the lamp, then stepped towards the armchair and the table by it. The smell of gas was heady now, and he bent down and turned off the tap.

He opened the cupboard just behind the chair, and saw two boxes of chocolates on a handy shelf. He picked them up, ripped off the top of the boxes, and saw the tell-tale blemishes on the smooth, dark surface of the bottom one. She did not eat a box full in one evening, that was just her joke.

Joke!

He put the drugged chocolates into his pocket, reminded himself that the others might have his prints on, and wiped them clean, then looked about very carefully, trying to make sure that he had left no clue. He searched the plain carpet and the bedspread and eiderdown for his own hairs, found two, took off his gloves to pick them up, and put them carefully on to his coat collar. He did not look much at the figure on the bed, but noticed that the sheet had fallen more closely to the shape of her head. He clenched his teeth and went close, pulling the sheet back, to find out whether she had loosened any of his hairs when beating at him; there were several, grey and wavy, actually on *her* hair.

He picked them off.

Steeling himself, he looked at her hands, and between the fingers of the right hand were more hairs.

He pulled these free.

He felt and heard his teeth grating as he turned away. He had to stand still for a minute before being steady enough to move. Then he drew on his gloves again, stepped to the door and listened carefully, heard nothing, and put out the main light. The bedside light hardly showed, and he hadn't the nerve to go back to switch it off. He pulled the door open stealthily, and the only sound was the rubbing against the carpet. A dim yellow glow shone at the head of the stairs, just outside the door. He closed the door again, holding his breath until it was closed tightly, and he waited for the click which would tell him that the latch was home; it seemed an age in coming, he ought to use his key. Then the click came very softly.

His heart was pounding.

He went down the stairs in the quiet, eerie house; there was no sound at all, not even of music, until he reached the ground floor. He heard a noise which alarmed him, and which he could not place at first; then he realised that it was a man snoring. He glared at the door. No light shone except that at the landing, to show latecomers the way.

He touched the handle of the front door, then heard a car engine. He drew back, snatching his hand away. It sounded like an old car, missing on one cylinder, and it was slowing down. He pressed tight against the wall behind the door. There was no doubt that it would stop near here, and might stop right outside. He moved away from the door and looked around desperately for a place to hide, but there was none; all the doors were locked, and each led to a small flat. There was Alice's room, but— He stood irresolute in the middle of the passage, and the car stopped, the engine stopped; then there was silence. He went closer to the door, ears straining for the slightest noise, but there was none. He bent down on one knee and tried to pull the letter-box open, but the spring was strong and he could not shift it. Without opening the door, there was no way of telling whether the car was just outside.

What the hell were they doing?

He drew back, staring longingly at the door handle, aching to open the door even an inch, but not daring to for at least five minutes. Five minutes, *what the hell were they doing?* He simply couldn't go back to Alice's room; he could not. His forehead and neck were clammy with sweat, the palms of his hands were moist and hot in those thin gloves.

The couple were necking, what else would they be doing? A couple in a car outside oblivious of—

There was a sound—a creaking—and the slamming of a door, followed by footsteps. A man said in a low-pitched voice:

"Won't be a jiffy, pet."

Pet, pet, pet—pet!

Another door opened. A girl spoke, but Payne could not hear the words. There was a sound of footsteps, very soft and confused, and then footsteps came slowly towards this door. Payne pressed himself against the wall behind it again. If it were thrust right back, it would squash him, and whoever opened it would know that someone was there. Would the man or the woman come in? The woman, of course, he was a fool to wonder. The woman—

A woman would be easier to handle, he thought; and he did not realise exactly what passed through his mind.

Why didn't they come?

The next sound was very close to the door, so close that it startled him.

The girl said: "No, sweetheart."

The man said: "I needn't stay long."

"I know, darling, but—"

"Ten minutes!"

"If you stay for ten minutes you'll stay all night, you know you will."

"It's what I want most in the world."

The girl said, with a soft-voiced insistence: "No, darling, we—we've got to wait."

"But why should we? We're going to get married soon, why should we—"

"Ted, darling, *please*."

In a flurry of panic, Payne thought that she was weakening; of course she would weaken, the man would get his own way. That meant the pair of them would come in, and would be bound to see him. He would have to fight. There would be two of the others, and he had no idea how powerful the man was. He stood absolutely rigid, hands clenched, feeling icily cold. Whispering was going on outside, and the little soft sounds of lovers; then the girl said:

"Ted, you must go."

"I don't want to go."

"I don't want you to, but you must."

"You're hard, honey!"

"We'll both be glad, in the morning."

"Don't you believe it!" the man exclaimed, in a louder voice than he had yet used. Payne detected a note of laughter in it, a rueful acknowledgment of defeat. Thank God for that! "Sweetheart."

"Yes?"

"Sure you won't change your mind?"

"Positive, darling."

"Hard, that's the word for you," the man insisted, but the laughter was louder in his voice. "Bless you! You couldn't be more right. But I must see you as far as your door."

No!

The girl laughed.

"I've seen you before," she said dryly. "There'll be a light on, and I'm perfectly capable of unlocking my own door, *thank you*. You can unlock this one for me, Sir Galahad."

Their mood had changed completely to one of light-hearted banter. The clever little bitch, Payne thought; she knew exactly how to handle the man—but there was still a possibility that he would insist, after all, that he was really playing the game his own way, that once the door was open, he would come in with her.

A key scraped on the latch; the girl laughed in a way that was almost a giggle. The key was inserted, and there was a sharp click. Payne pressed so tightly against the wall that the back of his head hurt, and he felt as if the pressure would soon pitch him forward. The door opened several inches, and the street light came through. The girl's voice sounded very much clearer.

"Good night, my darling."

"Good night, beloved."

He wasn't coming in—the girl had him where she wanted him. The door opened wider, but it didn't yet touch Payne. Wider still, until he could see shadows, and he felt the awful fear, that the man would make a last minute effort to have his way.

There was a rustle of sound, and a kiss, then a flurry of

movement. The girl stepped straight into the passage, with the door pressing hard against Payne's toes. She did not seem to notice.

The man's voice had a husky note.

"Good night."

Get it over, you lunatics, Payne breathed.

He was almost at screaming pitch. If the girl turned round this way to close the door, she could not fail to see him, and it was the natural way to turn. One scream before the door closed, and the man would rush in; one scream after it was closed, and the alarm would be raised. Payne could almost hear the man battering on the door, to come to the girl's rescue.

The girl turned the other way, so that she could look out for the last time, and whisper :

"Good night, darling."

"Good *night* !"

She closed the door. She stood by it for a moment, her back towards Payne. She could still turn this way, but every second was a help to Payne, for the man's footsteps sounded clearly. The other was losing no time, he would soon be at the car. What was this little fool doing? Was she going to open the door to have a last glimpse of him? Could anyone be so cloying, so—

She turned round, without facing him, and moved towards the stairs. He pressed against the corner, holding his breath. Her footsteps were soft, because she wore rubber soles. In this pale light, she looked young; she had rather long fair hair and wore a pale-coloured coat which was draped from her shoulders like a tent. She went straight to the stairs and started up them. Now the only danger was when she turned the bend in the stairs; if she looked round, she would be bound to see him, bound to scream.

He ought to go after her.

He could catch her up, and make sure that she couldn't raise the alarm.

The engine of the car started up, noisily. The girl hesi-

tated for a moment, and Payne thought she was going to turn.
Payne actually began to move forward, but instead of turning, she quickened her pace, rounded the bend in the stairs
and went up. Her head vanished, her shoulders, her body,
her shapely legs and feet.

The car moved off.

*　　*　　*

Cycling away from the adjoining street, Payne felt a
nausea which caused agony, and he began to say to himself :

"I would have killed her if she'd seen me. I would have
killed her."

4

SUSPECT

SUPERINTENDENT Roger West of the Criminal Investigation Department at New Scotland Yard woke a little before seven o'clock on the morning after the murder of Alice Murray. Janet, his wife, was snuggled close against him, with the eiderdown piled up on her; there was very little left for him, so there was a cold streak down his back. He edged a little closer to her, and promptly she edged away; he grinned. The cold streak was the argument for twin beds, the snugness the winning argument against them; they weren't likely to change until they were decrepit! He lay still for five minutes, then heard the clock strike in the front room downstairs. If he were sensible, he would get up now, shave and bathe, and bring Janet's tea in about half past seven; then there would be no need to hurry. He could call the boys at half past seven, too, and so create the outside possibility that Richard, the younger, would be ready for school without having to rush.

But this was comfortable; cosy; seductive.

He slid his arm round Janet, suspecting that she was between waking and sleeping; it was a pity to make her wake up earlier than she must. He made the effort, and got out of bed; brrrh! This house was like an icebox in the cold spells. He thought again, as he often did these days, that it was time they moved, when they did the new house must have central heating. Why did the English pretend that it was an invention of the frail and sickly?

He slid his arms into the sleeves of a woollen dressing-gown, and went out. The boys' door was closed. That was another reason for wanting to move; they really needed a room each at fifteen and sixteen, yet if they had it, the spare room would go, and there would be no room for friends and relations. Fifteen and sixteen—good lord! And he and Janet had been here for five years before Martin had come along. Twenty-one years in the same place, and with much of the same furniture; no wonder he felt that they wanted a change, and no wonder Janet was beginning to revolt against paint and patching.

The house had been suitable for a detective sergeant, even a detective inspector, and just passable for a chief inspector—but it wasn't good enough for a chief superintendent.

Roger shaved and had his bath, went downstairs, and was putting the kettle on when the telephone bell rang. He hurried into the front room to answer it, as always wishing that he had a telephone extension in the kitchen. Why was it that he could keep putting off an essential thing like that? He went into the front room, the sitting-room-cum-parlour, and the curtains were drawn, there was a slightly stale smell of tobacco smoke, making him wrinkle his nose. He put on the light and grabbed the receiver.

"West speaking."

"Sorry to worry you, Mr. West." This was the traditional piece of nonsense if he was being called out when not on duty. "But Mr. Sloan would like a word with you."

Bill Sloan, recently promoted to superintendency, was on night duty; and he would not call Roger unless there was really a good reason.

"Put him through," Roger said, and there was only a moment's pause before Sloan came on with his deep voice holding an occasional undertone of Cockney. Roger could picture this big, red-faced man who was beginning to put on weight.

"Morning, Roger," Sloan greeted. "How would you like a nice little job right on your doorstep?"

"What job?" Roger asked cautiously.

"Murder," answered Sloan briefly. "A girl strangled round in Manville Street. See what I mean by saying it's on your doorstep?"

Roger said: "Yes, Bill, thanks." Sloan knew that if he took over an inquiry so close home as this, he would be able to slip indoors for meals and look in during the day; it was a piece of cake which seldom came a Yard man's way, and characteristic of Sloan to make sure that he had a chance at it.

"If you get along right away, you're bound to be handed the job," Sloan said.

"I will. Who's there now?"

"Freddy Thompson, of the Division, and he's been bleating for help. We only had the flash ten minutes ago. I don't even know how the body was discovered yet. Freddy's due off at eight, and he'll be glad to unload everything on to you."

"Okay," Roger said. "Tell him I'll be there in a quarter of an hour or so, will you?"

"Needn't break your neck," Sloan told him. "Or were you up and about?"

"Just up," Roger said. "What's this girl's name?"

"Dunno. The address is 24, Manville Street, and it's an apartment house."

"A flatlet house," Roger corrected, thoughtfully. "I know the place. Thanks again, Bill."

"Forget it," Sloan said, and chuckled. "Don't make it last too long!"

He rang off.

Roger made the tea, and was carrying it upstairs when Richard, tall, thin, with an unruly mop of dark hair, a very clear, fresh complexion and blue eyes which looked huge and sleepy, was coming out of the bathroom.

"Morning, Dad."

"Morning, little 'un. How's tricks?"

"Fine, thanks."

"The catarrh?"

"Haven't been awake long enough to know," answered Richard, "but I think it's getting better."

"Keep at the exercises and the tablets," Roger urged. "You'll beat it if you work hard. How's the big 'un?"

"Still in bed," Richard answered.

"Oh, no, he isn't," observed Martin—called Scoopy—in a sepulchral voice. He put his head round his bedroom door, which was close to the bathroom. "I've been up for at least twenty-seven seconds. Morning, Dad. Was that a case?"

"Yes."

"Murder?"

"Yes."

"I *hate* murders," Richard declared with sudden shrillness. "Why do people have to *kill* people?" He stood rubbing his eyes, pyjama trousers gaping unashamedly, jacket fastened at the wrong buttons, looking worried and indignant. Martin came into full view, naked except for a pair of short pants, a little taller, much broader and much more powerful than his brother, hair between colours and much more untidy. His chest was massive—already forty-one to Roger's forty-four. He threw out his chest and pummelled it, saying:

"You want me to deal with them, that's what you want! I'd give 'em murder!"

"You put something on or you'll die of cold," Roger said. He hesitated, aware of Richard staring at him intently; Richard never gave up without getting some kind of answer to any question he posed, and here was a question which should be answered. "Fish," Roger said, "you remember when you were younger, you used to get into flaming tempers?"

"Yes, Dad."

"He used to think he could fight *me*," Scoopy remarked, grinning.

"Some people lose their temper far worse than you did, they commit murder as a result, and spend the rest of their lives wishing they hadn't," Roger said. "Others get frightened of being found out in some crime, and kill to save themselves. Others get greedy."

This wasn't very good, but it seemed to satisfy Richard for the moment, for he said :

"Oh, I see."

Scoopy grinned.

"Well, that's more than I do."

"You get washed," Roger ordered, and smothered a grin as he turned round with the tea tray. It didn't surprise him to see Janet sitting up in bed, dressing jacket wrapped tightly round her shoulders, hair net already off; her dark hair was beginning to turn grey. She had a very clear complexion and always looked fresh in the mornings. "Hallo," Roger greeted. "So you can wake up."

"Have you got to go out already?" Janet asked, as he leaned forward and kissed her.

"Only round the corner," he answered. "I'll be back for breakfast."

Ten minutes later, he was out of the house, one of many detached ones in Bell Street, each with its well matured garden, neat hedge and winter-trim lawn. At the first corner was the largest house in the street, exactly right for him and Janet, and he had heard rumours that it was for sale. Would the price be too high? He paused, heard a whistle, looked round and saw the boys waving from the main bedroom window. Two neighbours were passing on the way to the buses in King's Road, and there was a flutter of good mornings. Two paper boys were standing by their bicycles, in earnest consultation. A small girl with ridiculous spike-heeled shoes and over-painted lips and cheeks closed the door of a house at the corner, and came hurrying along the garden path, obviously late for her bus. She glanced at Roger and he said : "Good morning."

"Good morning, superintendent !"

Roger turned the corner, his back to the girl, and saw two police cars and three policemen standing outside 24, Manville Street. Although it was just round the corner from Bell Street where he lived, the houses here had a different style and character. These were fifty years older, and stood in a terrace, all of them five storeys high. Number 24 was two houses made into one, and thirty years ago a fairly good job of conversion had been done. The landlord and his wife lived in a basement flat approached from the entrance to Number 22, and the main flatlets were approached by the single staircase of Number 24. It was an advantage to know the layout in advance. A uniformed man recognised Roger, saluted, and waved two excited-looking schoolboys away. Roger turned into Number 24, seeing the narrow passage and hearing voices, including those of a querulous, scared-sounding woman. Then he heard Thompson's deep voice. Thompson was a senior superintendent in his last years at the Division. For some reason, he had always preferred night duty. He was a massive barrel of a man dressed in crumpled brown, and was talking to a dumpy grey-haired woman who still had curlers in her hair.

"But I keep telling you," the woman said. "I just happened to be awake early and I'd run out of milk. I popped down to see if the milkman had been but he hadn't and I was coming upstairs. Then I saw a light at Miss Murray's door, the door wasn't quite closed you see, it often springs open if it's closed from the outside, her door does, the lock needs attention. I thought she wouldn't mind lending me a little milk if she was awake, so I tapped, and when there wasn't any answer I pushed the door a little wider, wondering if she was all right, and then I *saw* her."

It was a good, straightforward, breathlessly told story.

Thompson said: "Thank you, Mrs Cartwright. I won't need to worry you any more just now. You'll be in for the next hour, won't you?"

"I'll be in all the *morning*," Mrs. Cartwright declared, and turned to see who Thompson was staring at. She looked into Roger's eyes, and he saw the defensiveness in hers; she was afraid that he was going to ask her to repeat what she had said.

He smiled, not knowing that it was the way he did so, and his briskness, which had helped to earn him the nickname 'Handsome'; that had stuck during his twenty-five years at the Yard.

"Did you get any milk, Mrs. Cartwright?" he asked.

"Did I—" The woman opened her mouth wide, and then said in vexation: "Would you believe it, I completely *forgot*."

"Not really surprising," Roger said lightly, and turned and called to the constable just outside the front door. "Rustle up a pint of milk, constable, the milkman's just along the street."

Mrs. Cartwright managed to say: "Thank you *everso*," as Roger passed her. Thompson was smiling behind his heavy moustache. Roger winked, and they went upstairs, Roger in the lead because the staircase was not wide enough for two such massive men.

"Public relations, that ought to be your field," Thompson declared. "You'd have them eating out of your hand. How are tricks?"

"We live."

"That what you call it?" Thompson asked with heavy sarcasm. There was little humour in his rather heavy-lidded brown eyes. "Got a nasty one here, Handsome. Wondered if Sloan would give it to you." He pointed upwards. "One more flight." A minute later, Roger stepped into the one-room flatlet where the dead girl lay on the bed, and three Yard men were taking measurements showing the position of the bed in relation to the doors, window and furniture. Another man was fiddling with a camera on a tripod. The Yard could be as old fashioned as a small county force. "Here she is," Thompson said, needlessly. "Named Murray —Alice Murray."

"Sent for a doctor?"

"On the way."

"Anyone touched her?"

"Nope." Thompson moved towards an outflung arm. "I felt her pulse, that's all. Cold already."

"Stiff?"

"Yes."

"Been dead some time, then," Roger observed. He stood

looking down at the oval face of the girl, seeing the now dark bruises at her throat, seeing also the odd angle of her neck. Could there be a broken neck as well as strangulation? The police surgeon would have the last word about that.

The girl looked quite charming as she lay there. Her dark hair was short, with the rather untidy kind of cut that some girls thought was attractive, and she had very ordinary features, but a fine complexion.

"We had any luck?" Roger asked.

"Not a thing, yet," Thompson answered. "But we haven't had much time, Handsome, give us a chance. What would you like to do?"

"It's your case," Roger said.

"Only for another two and a half minutes," Thompson declared, taking a big gold watch out of his waistcoat pocket. "Don't mind me, you won't tread on my toes."

"Have it your own way," said Roger. "We'll have the room vacuumed as soon as we can, but have a look round for obvious things first. Didn't send for Fox, did you?"

"He's on days."

"We have to have some luck," Roger said, and turned to one of the detectives who was busy with measuring tape, pad and pencil. "Go down and radio the Yard for Detective Sergeant Fox and his bag of tricks, will you?" he asked. "Speak to Mr. Sloan. He'll still be there, and he'll fix it." Roger looked at Thompson. "How many chaps can you spare for questioning everyone in the house and in the street?"

"Half a dozen, I s'pose."

"I'll get another half a dozen from the Yard," Roger said. "We don't want to lose any time. The tenants won't like it, but no one must leave the house until we give the okay. Anyone tried to leave?" he inquired.

"Not yet, but Mrs. Cartwright said there are two people who left at about a quarter past seven."

"Pity," said Roger. "We'll find out where they work

from the landlord, though, that shouldn't be much trouble."
He was thinking exactly what should be done, and what
reaction to expect from anyone inconvenienced by the investigation. In the next half hour, most of the residents
would want to leave for their offices and shops, there would
be protest and possibly uproar when they were detained.
The daily exodus would start any minute, and the best way
of making sure there wasn't a build-up was to station a man
at each landing, and keep the residents there as they opened
the doors of their flats.

"Drop those jobs," Roger said to the two men in the
room, "and take over a landing apiece. Be very nice and
polite, but tell everyone they can't come out, and ask them
if they heard anything—all the usual routine. Don't forget
to lay on the honey."

Thompson said : "I'll go and bring a couple more of my
chaps up, Handsome." He went out, leaving Roger alone
with the body of the girl. He stood looking down at her, and
then very gently turned the sheet down farther from her
chin. He saw the pyjamas hugging the almost adolescent
curves of the breasts, the legs drawn up a little, but there
was nothing to suggest that this girl had fought hard, or that
anyone had attempted to rape her; one good thing. He
studied the angle of the neck again, saw the bruises, saw
that the right arm was flung out, almost straight. He could
imagine that she had been disturbed, put on the light, and
been attacked as she did so. This had the look of a burglar
having been caught by surprise, but what would a burglar
think was worth taking from here? No one with any money
or valuables would live in this kind of house, so the obvious
solution had a self-evident snag. Obvious things too often
had. He moved to the window and opened the curtains an
inch or two. It was a bright morning and would soon be
broad daylight; when Fox arrived, he could make his search
by the naked eye first, and then get busy with his vacuum
cleaner. Fox was the best man at the Yard for a room
search, a man who could spot even split hairs.

Thompson came back. "That's fixed, every landing's watched, and the first squawk made," he said. "Old Dammit is coming up the stairs, he won't waste any time." Old Dammit was the affectionate nickname for Dr. Claude Mortimer, the chief divisional police surgeon. "I'm going back to clear up at the office. All right?"

Roger looked straight at him.

"The girl didn't get out of bed, so she didn't open the door. She wouldn't be likely to go to bed with it open. If he'd picked the lock we'd know—that lock was turned with a key. So, it was someone who had a key. Boy friend, lover, brother, sister, girl friend, that's who we're after."

"You know your trouble," growled Thompson. "You think too fast. If you ask me, the best witness for your money is Mrs. Nosey Cartwright, if she would push open a neighbour's door like that—" Thompson broke off, and grinned, his eyes widening. "Oh, I see, that's why you fixed her up with some milk! Crafty so-and-so, that's what you are. I'll be seeing you, Handsome. Happy the case is in good hands!"

He grinned again and went off, to bump into Claude Mortimer at the door.

"Dammit," Mortimer complained, "you don't have to tread on my toes."

"Sorry, Doc."

"Morning, Doc," Roger greeted. "Couldn't be more glad to see you. Mind having a look at this, while I have a word with a neighbour who might have heard something?"

"Pleasure to have you out of my way," Mortimer declared. He was a short, paunchy man, breathless from the stairs, always inclined to be crotchety, but a very able police surgeon who worked quickly and who seldom gave an opinion which wasn't subsequently confirmed by an autopsy or evidence. "Oh dear, oh dear," he said as he looked at the girl. "Dammit, why *do* these things have to happen?"

Roger went across to Mrs. Cartwright's door, and was not surprised when it opened the moment he tapped; she must have been listening intently. Nor was he surprised that she had a fund of knowledge about the tenants, or that she knew that once or twice Alice Murray had had a man in her room, or that she *believed* she knew who the man was.

A rather young, bald-headed man, ever so well dressed, who had a Jaguar car. She couldn't be sure, of course, but this man had driven her home sometimes; he had never come in, but young people were so cunning these days, weren't they? Why, Miss Murray had even called the man Mr. Something, not by his first name, although the man had called her Alice. A smooth type, if Roger knew what she meant, and the name—oh, yes, she remembered the name, it was *Anderson*. So unapt, if he knew what she meant!

*   *   *

Mrs. Cartwright also knew that Alice worked for a jewel merchant named Anderson, who had a shop in Kensington High Street.

5

LATE MORNING

JOHN PAYNE felt a tug at his shoulder, waking him out of the stupor of sleep. On the instant he felt the kind of panic which had seized him several times last night; his body went rigid, he kept his eyes tightly closed, almost afraid to see who was shaking him.

Then, Gwen said: "What on earth is the matter with us this morning?"

The laugh, never far away from her, sounded in her voice—like that of the man, last night. Payne opened his eyes slowly, and looked at her through his lashes, anxious that she should not see the expression in his eyes at first. She was wearing a dressing-gown, her flaxen hair was very fluffy, as if she'd just run a comb through it, and she had on no make up. She was bending over and shaking him.

"Hallo, Gwen," he mumbled. "Is it late?"

"Late? It's ten o'clock."

"*What?*" he exclaimed, and opened his eyes wide at last. "It can't be!"

"It is," Gwen insisted. "Goodness knows why, but we've all overslept. Thank goodness it's Saturday, and only Hilda has to go early."

"Good lord!" Payne said, and hitched himself up in his pillows. The bedside clock showed that it was a little after ten. "We haven't done this for months."

"And then only after a late night," said Gwen. "It must have been that sausage toad."

"But we've had—" Payne began, and then broke off, seeing her smiling at him. "Well, it doesn't matter what caused it, we've overslept."

"Did you have anything special to do this morning?" Gwen asked.

"I wanted to see a couple of customers, but it wasn't urgent, and I had no appointments. Just as well," Payne added, "we might as well make a morning of it, now."

"You can if you like, but I've got to go and do the shopping," Gwen said. "Maurice wants an early lunch, he's playing football at Harrow this afternoon, and the kick off is at two. Like breakfast in bed?"

"Er—no," decided Payne. "No, I'll have a cup of tea, and then get up. You forget all about me, I'll get what I want to eat."

"Please yourself, duckie." Gwen stood back, looking at him, and he was uneasily aware of the broad daylight on his face; the sun was much brighter than most winter mornings. "Are you feeling all right, Jack?"

"Bit heady, that's all," Payne said. "I slept too long."

"What time did you come to bed?"

"Soon after midnight."

"You look as if you hardly slept at all," Gwen remarked. "I'd lay in, if I were you." She drew back, and Payne was glad when she turned and was no longer looking at him. Her dressing-gown was tied tightly round the waist, and nothing ever disguised her swaying walk, but he was not thinking about Gwen and her curves. He was thinking of the restless hours he had spent here; the dread of waking her when he had first come home; the way he had undressed and crept into his cold bed; the way he had tried to sleep, but had been haunted by Alice's face. It would not have mattered if he had left Alice sleeping, but to know that she had been aware of what he was doing, that her last few minutes alive had been in awful fear, was the haunting horror.

He wanted to be alone.

His head ached, and when he leaned forward to see his face in the mirror, he could understand why Gwen had been so concerned. His eyes were bloodshot, and his skin pasty.

Shock of course—it would be a long time before he recovered from the ordeal of the night. If that couple of love
birds hadn't come when they had, he might have been all
right, but it had been a long drawn out agony.

At least no one would even know he had been out; no one
could connect him with Alice . . .

Could they?

Had he been careful enough?

He tried to tell himself that there was nothing to worry
about, but fears which had not even occurred to him before the murder crowded his mind, and suddenly he
shivered. He would have to get over this mood, Gwen would
soon begin to suspect that there was a guilty reason for it.
He got up, went to the bathroom, and washed vigorously.
Cold water stung some colour back to his cheeks, but his
eyes remained bloodshot. When he got back to the bedroom,
Gwen was coming up the stairs with the tea tray, and Hilda
called out :

" 'Bye, Mum ! 'Bye, Dad !"

"Off you go," Gwen called.

" *'Bye!*" Payne made himself shout, and his head pounded
after the exertion. "She'll be in trouble," he said to Gwen.
"They hate her being late on Saturday mornings."

"Well, they'll have to lump it," Gwen declared, and put
the tray down and studied him again. "Are you sure you
feel all right? You look a bit flushed. I'll pop into the bathroom and get the thermometer, see if you're running a temperature."

He shouted : "Don't fuss me ! I'm perfectly all right !"

Gwen stared in astonishment; it was months, perhaps
years, since he had raised his voice at her.

"You *must* be feeling bad," she observed drily. "I don't
care what you say, I'm going to take your temperature." She
put the tray down and went out, leaving Payne lying back
on his pillows, frightened at himself. To shout at *Gwen.* He
felt perspiration cold on his forehead, and on his neck. He
strained up so as to look at his reflection, and saw the flush

receding, pallor replacing it; no wonder she thought he was ill.

He must get a hold on himself, and tell her something, anything, which would help to explain that outburst. But his head ached so much. Without warning, Maurice began to whistle on a high pitched note; he wanted to scream at the boy. A door banged. Payne clenched his teeth. Maurice came walking and whistling along, saw the bedroom door wide open, looked in and flicked a salute.

"Morning, Pop!"

"Hallo, Maurice," Payne said.

"Say, what's the matter with *you*?"

"Maurice," Gwen called, "your father isn't well this morning. Stop that whistling and go downstairs and start cooking the breakfast."

"Sure," said Maurice, promptly, and his face was a study in concern. "Sorry you're not well, Dad. It's nothing serious, is it?"

"Of course it isn't," his mother declared, bustling along from the bathroom. "It's something we ate last night."

"I feel fine, now I am awake," Maurice said, and looked hard at his father, then turned and walked quietly away. At the foot of the stairs, he began to whistle, softly for him.

Gwen sat at the side of the bed.

"Let's take this temperature before you drink hot tea," she said, and Payne opened his mouth like a small boy.

In a way, Gwen had always seemed older than he, although they were the same age almost to the month. She looked years younger because of her smooth skin, and there was only a hint of lines at her eyes. She had a natural merriness which made her extremely popular with nearly everyone who knew her. Payne believed that she was truly a happy woman, not even disappointed because he had failed to make good his boasts of what he would do for her and the family. In a way her lighthearted comments on their modest income had made him keep longing for success. He had never been able to bear being laughed at, even good-naturedly, even by Gwen.

She watched him with her head on one side, obviously his outburst had amused more than annoyed her, as he should have known. The thermometer seemed to become larger, and he kept wanting to gulp. It was a relief when she took the thing out, turned towards the window, and read it; she was frowning as she twisted it this way and that, then her face cleared and she said :

"It's as near normal as can be."

"Of course it is," Payne said, gruffly. "I've got a shocking headache, that's all. I—" Suddenly, the 'explanation' came to him, surely enough to make her think she knew what had put that harshness into his voice, yet something that could easily be laughed off. "Gwen, I'm sorry, but—you won't laugh?"

She chuckled.

"I can't promise that!"

That made him smile, and also made his heart lighter.

"I had the most god-awful dream," he declared. "I can't tell you exactly what it was about, but—but Hilda and Maurice were somehow mixed up in it, and there were gravestones and headstones." He took her hand. "Kick me if I behave like that again."

"It must have been beastly," Gwen said. She took him more seriously than he had expected, and he wasn't really surprised when she went on : "It's a funny thing, but Hilda has had several nightmares lately. I've put it down to her age, but once she woke up screaming—that night you were in Bournemouth."

"We must watch her," Payne said. "Must be a reason for it."

Gwen poured out tea, then began to dress. Payne lay back, watching. Her figure could stir him to desire and to passion now as quickly as it had in their early days, and she had a boldness, almost a brazenness, as if she deliberately set out to hold his gaze and to stir his desire. He watched as she put her hands behind her back, to fasten her bra; the ends slipped and the bra dropped. She pursed her lips as if in vexation, but the gleam of humour, of enticement, was unmistakable in her eyes. Suddenly he seemed to picture Alice Murray by her side. Oh, God, it was funny. *Funny!* He actually wanted to laugh. He drank his tea, put the cup down, and said :

"Strip tease over ?"

"This performance," Gwen said, then wriggled into a dress which clung to her figure, came over to the bed, kissed him lightly on the forehead, and said : "Lie in for the morning, anyhow. Business can wait."

"Business can never wait," Payne rejoined, and in the lighter mood, he went on buoyantly : "As a matter of fact, sweetie-pie, it's picking up extremely well. I've one or two big deals which might make us a fortune."

"You and your fortune, it's always round the corner," Gwen scoffed. "Just make enough to get us out of this house and buy me a mink stole, and I'll admit you're a better business man than I thought you were."

"Before we've finished, you shall have a mink coat which drags on the ground, and a Rolls-Royce to go with the new house," Payne declared earnestly.

"I'll settle for a Jaguar." Gwen was still joking, without malice but hurtfully. If only she knew what he had done for her! She stood with the tray in her hands, looking down at him. "You look twice the man you did already. The next time you have a nightmare, tell me about it right away."

"Take it from me I will," Payne said.

There wasn't going to be a next time. There was going to be the theft from Anderson's, followed by a series of business deals, all carefully arranged to show substantial profits in his books. He would 'win' one or two good bets, too; nothing excessive, nothing to attract attention, but a hundred pounds or so at a time, to build up his bank balance gradually. There was no end to what he could do once he had that stock from Andersons. If he chose a Friday night, there would be the better part of two thousand pounds in cash, to go with it.

He lazed until lunch-time, felt quite himself again when he went downstairs, and could think of Alice without panic or alarm. It was a pity it had happened the way it had, but she had only suffered for a minute or two, and it was even possible that she hadn't known who was attacking her.

She was dead; buried in the past. Now he had to make his future.

In this new mood of confidence, it did not occur to him seriously that the police would ever catch up, but when he went out, about six o'clock that evening, to get some cigarettes and the classified football edition of the evening newspapers, tension suddenly gripped him again. On most Saturday evenings the family sat round the television, with a sandwich supper, a comfortable armchair for everyone, and Gwen was getting it ready. Payne was alone, and desperately full of disquiet. He kept a look-out for Hilda, who usually got home by half past six but occasionally arrived half an hour earlier. He hoped that he would not meet her tonight—certainly not until he had seen the newspaper.

He bought the *Evening Globe*. Instead of looking for the Fulham result, he stared at the headlines. There had been a serious plane crash near Paris; there had been an avalanche in Scotland, and two climbers were missing; and there had been a murder in south-west London.

He stood quite still, reading about it. How Alice's murder had been discovered, how the police had arrived at once, how Superintendent Roger West of New Scotland Yard was in charge of the investigations, and how :

> *Mr. Julian Anderson, son of the owner of the jewel merchant for whom the dead girl worked, may have information of value to the police.*

Payne's head jerked up.

"My God!" he breathed. "When they say that, they usually mean they want the devil! Julian, the swine!" He began to laugh, actually laughed aloud, and made several people turn round to stare; a man said half jokingly:

"Got your treble chance right, mate?"

"Pulled—pulled off four draws," Payne made himself answer. He mustn't let himself get out of hand. What he wanted was a couple of stiff whiskies, that would put him right, and there was no need to keep off drink now, these could be the doubles he had promised himself. One in the pub and a couple at home. If the spectacular show on television was good tonight, he could laugh as much as he wanted to; he could be positively hilarious! He folded the newspaper and tucked it under his arm, thinking again of Julian Anderson, and how Alice had disliked him, how he had actually tried to follow her last night! Although Alice had been too nice-natured to say so, there wasn't much doubt that Julian was a man who encouraged his hands to stray. He looked the type.

This would teach him!

Payne strode towards the local public house, the King's Arms in the High Street, saw a bus pull up at the stop opposite, and caught sight of Hilda. Waving, she jumped off the bus and came to him eagerly, trustingly; again she reminded him of Alice, although physically she was so different.

"Hallo, Dad! Been getting your paper?"

"Yes. Nothing turned up on the pools," he answered.

"Our ship will come home one of these days."

She turned to walk beside him, and reminded him of Gwen when she had been younger. Gwen had had the same flamboyant figure and had flaunted it perhaps a little more; or perhaps it had seemed more, in those days. Payne decided to wait for the whisky until he got home, it was a bad thing to encourage a girl of eighteen to go into pubs. Hilda would start that soon enough with boy friends. It was good to have her walking alongside him, chattering about the day at the shop—she worked in a mantle and gown shop in Hammersmith—about television, about the way they had overslept, and how Mrs. Cowley—the manager—had been quite rude about it. As they walked on, Payne noticed how many men, young and old, looked at her, some of them covertly, some with open admiration. Well, that wasn't surprising. Gwen would be able to give her all the tuition she needed! The thought made him frown. How much did he, how much did Gwen, really know about their own daughter?

". . . Oh, I remember what I was going to say to you. I don't suppose you've seen the evening paper yet," said Hilda. "You remember Anderson's, the place where you used to work years ago?"

Payne said, stiffly, heart turning over: "Yes."

Hilda did not notice the strangeness of his voice, and went on without a pause:

"A terrible thing happened, absolutely awful. Mr. Anderson's secretary was murdered last night. I wonder if she was there when you were, Dad. Her name was Marshall, I think, Alice Marshall, or Marbel, or something like that. I read it in the *Star*. And it *looks* as if Anderson's son did it. You used to say what a nasty piece of work Julian Anderson was, didn't you? His name *was* Julian, wasn't it?"

Payne said, more normally: "Yes. What a dreadful thing." As they walked along, he realised that he should have been prepared for this, and that it was a good thing that Hilda, not Gwen, had come out with the story. Gwen would have noticed the way it affected him.

He wondered where Julian Anderson was now.

6

STATEMENTS

CHARLEY FOX was a little man by the standards of the
Metropolitan Police, and just young enough to have
squeezed in when the regulation height had been lowered
to five feet eight inches. He was not only small, but thin,
bony and ugly, and his shoulders were slightly rounded. On
the only occasion when Roger had seen him stripped, just
after an investigation when they had been caught out in a
heavy rain storm, he had been astonished by Fox's powerful
chest, biceps and forearms; all these were over-developed,
and his arms were very long, giving him almost a simian
appearance. His ugliness was monkey-like, too. But he had
the sharpest pair of eyes in the Force, and his power of observation of physical things had marked out a course for
him.

He called himself chief of the Dry Cleaning Department
at the Yard.

His main job was to examine the scene of a crime for
anything which might be used as evidence, but he also
cleaned clothes, examined boots and shoes, studied the art
of finding things which nine men out of ten would have
missed. Generally, this was all he was expected to do. Roger
West, studying him that morning, and watching the way he
considered all aspects of the case, wondered whether Fox
had ambitions to get out of the rut in which he could never
hope to get beyond detective inspector's level.

He briefed Fox to look for anything in the room or between the room and the front door of Number 24, and then
went out to face the sarcasm, the annoyance, the anxiety
and the impatience of eleven residents who wanted to leave
at once, and who were already late for work. There was a

girl, almost in tears, saying that if she were late she would almost certainly lose her job. There was an elderly man, bowler-hatted and carrying a furled black umbrella, who said in tones of abject misery :

"I have not been late *once* in thirty-four years."

"Time he was," a detective sergeant named Noble muttered to Roger.

Roger said : "If it will help, I will arrange to have all your employers telephoned officially and told that the delay has been caused by us, and that we will see that you get away just as soon as possible."

The little girl gasped : "If only you *would* !"

"That would be very considerate of you," said the bowler-hatted man, perking up. "I am sure that it would not then be registered against me, and if it were an *official* message—"

"Collect all the telephone numbers, and get that laid on," Roger instructed Noble, ignoring the man's look of disgust.

Then Roger began to question the neighbours, and soon had cause to wonder whether he would get far. No one appeared to have heard anything unusual during the night except a middle-aged physiotherapist who looked vaguely like a circus lion-tamer, and who had heard 'something fall' in the flat below her at about a quarter to one. It might have been half past twelve or even a little earlier, she admitted, but she had been in bed for a while, after turning in about midnight. A nice-looking, fresh-faced girl with long, fair hair, who wore a tight fitting black jumper with a high neck and long sleeves, and the latest kind of elasticised, figure-fit slacks, volunteered a little hesitantly :

"I came in about half past eleven, sir."

"Did you notice anything unusual?" asked Roger mechanically. He saw that the girl was a little ill-at-ease, then noticed that an older woman was looking down her nose in apparent disapproval.

"Well, no, I didn't really," the girl said.

"I wonder if you'll spare me five minutes a little later,"

Roger said. "May I come to your room?" The girl went off with obvious relief. He finished with all the others, and promised that they would be able to leave immediately the police had finished the search of the staircase and the hall. Then he checked what Fox was doing.

Fox was bending over the dead girl's body, which was now completely covered, and plucking at something on the pillow with a pair of tweezers.

"What?" asked Roger.

"Hairs, Mr. West."

"Not hers?"

"Grey as a badger's."

"Keep it up," Roger said. "Had any other luck?"

"Not a sausage. Not in my department, anyhow."

Roger stood by the door.

"Any department?"

"Well," Fox said, a little hesitantly, "I watched them taking the pictures and I heard what Old Dammit said, but no one noticed what I think I did. The thumb marks on the neck. The strangler must have been standing about where you are, and lunged forward at her. The way she's lying against the head panel you'd think his right hand would be higher than the other, and the pressure would be from her left side to her right, wouldn't you?"

"Yes."

"Well, it wasn't—her neck was bent the other way," Fox said.

"Translate it, will you?" Roger asked.

"Sure you need me to?"

"Sure, I want to know if you can!"

Fox grinned; he was more attractive when he smiled than when in a serious mood.

"Well, that left hand went higher and used a lot more force. I'd lay odds the chap was left-handed."

"Chap?"

"Don't imagine it could have been a woman, do you?" said Fox, astonished. "I shouldn't have—" He broke off, turned his eyes towards the ceiling, and said: "Strewth! There's a physiotherapist upstairs with bulging muscles. She could, I suppose. Any reason to think she did?"

"None at all," Roger said. "Just reason to wonder if it's safe to take it for granted that it was a man. Keep at it, Charley."

"About finished, except that I've got to vacuum clean the carpet," declared Fox. "I did manage to get onto the stairs and the passage pretty quick. There's one thing you could do for me, Mr. West."

"What's that?"

"Let me get the vacuum busy before half a dozen other yobs stamp about the place," pleaded Fox. "I'll bet I'll find dust or bits of dirt from a dozen different places, most of them from our chaps' shoes. Hell of job when it's as complicated as that. I know everyone wants to get here first, but it's worth thinking about."

"I'll see if I can lay it on," said Roger. "Did you find anything on the staircase?"

"Nope."

"Pity," Roger sympathised. "I'll be seeing you." He hurried down the stairs and into the street, where a Divisional detective inspector was organising door-to-door calls by the police to find out which people living nearby had been awake at midnight or after. That was another chore which would not be popular but could not be avoided. Several neighbours had been up and were now being questioned, and the Divisional man said:

"'There's one description of a chap who brought the girl home in a Jaguar sometimes, Mr. West."

"Reliable?" asked Roger.

"Well, I've got it from three neighbours," the other told him. "It was a black Jaguar, probably a 1957, Mark VII, and the man was shortish, bald headed—he didn't wear a hat—and rather broad."

"Did he ever go in?"

"He wasn't seen to."

"Keep at it," Roger urged.

It was then nearly half past nine, he was feeling hungry, and was acutely conscious of the number of things that he wanted to do; among them, go to Anderson's shop in Kensington, where the girl worked and where the Andersons—her employers—lived in a flat above the shop. He had talked to the Yard, and a Detective Inspector Gill and a couple of sergeants had gone to the shop to start questioning the staff, and to find out if anything was missing, but he wanted to be there himself as soon as he could. He went into the murder-house again, and found the girl in the close fitting slacks and jumper waiting for him in a room at the top of the building. This was Jennifer Ling, according to the list of residents Noble had prepared. She had a slim figure rather like that of the dead girl, and a fresh, wholesome look. There was an appetising odour of bacon which made Roger feel more hungry than ever, and the girl was buttering a slice of toast.

"I'm very grateful that you didn't question me in front of the others," she said, and Roger liked her smile and her frankness. "There's a friend of my mother in one of the other flats, and she tittle-tattles so much you wouldn't believe. Actually, I was in about *one* o'clock."

"Did you notice anything?"

"Well, yes," the girl said hesitantly. "I saw that there was some light at Alice Murray's door, it wasn't properly closed. I—but would you like a cup of coffee?"

"Nice of you," Roger said. "Yes, thanks."

"I've just made it, and I put an extra spoonful in, in case," the girl said. "I thought you might have been on duty since the early hours." She poured out, obviously doing all this to cover her nervousness, as most people were nervous when talking to the police. "Sugar?" she asked.

"Thanks."

"I hope it's as you like it," Jennifer Ling went on. "The truth is, I've seen the door like that once or twice. I don't think it closes properly unless you slam it, and there are times when you don't want to slam it. I—I get in very late sometimes, as late as two and three o'clock, if I go dancing."

"Have you ever seen a man in the room with Miss Murray?" asked Roger. This was probably what she wanted to tell him, but wanted to be led.

"Well, I did *once*." Jennifer spread her hands. "Actually I'd come in late, and thought I heard something so I looked downstairs, and a man was leaving her flat."

"Was that the only time you saw him?"

"Yes."

"And the only man you've seen leaving or entering her flat?"

"Yes, although sometimes Julian Anderson brings her home," Jennifer reported. "He's the son of the man she works for, and he's always hanging around. The trouble with Alice," went on the girl, jumping up and walking about the room on her toes, "is that she was too kind-hearted. She just couldn't tell him where to get off."

"And he needed telling?"

"He needed telling all right!" Now, Jennifer moved to the window and stood looking at Roger, slender, black-clad legs close together and rising on her toes, rather like a silhouette of a dancer seen on a coloured screen. "But he wasn't the man I saw leaving Alice's room, I—oh, I feel an utter beast talking about her like this."

"You needn't," Roger said. "You might get us to the killer before he can kill someone else."

"You mean—"

"I mean what I say," Roger assured her; there was no better way of making sure that the girl would hold nothing back. "What was this second man like?"

"I'm honestly not sure," the girl answered, "but there was something about him which suggested he wasn't young —not a boy, anyhow. He was rather tall, and wearing a trilby hat. I heard him whisper good night to Alice, and then he went downstairs. He didn't hurry, but walked rather stealthily. Do you know what I mean?"

"I wish all witnesses were half as good," Roger praised. "And I hope you've something else for me."

"I have and I haven't," said Jennifer Ling, "but I *think* I saw Alice with a man a few weeks ago. He was middle-aged, rather handsome as a matter of fact, and very well dressed. They were going into a cinema together, and I was passing. Alice saw me but didn't wave or anything, so I assumed that she didn't want me to take any notice."

"Was it the man you saw here?"

"I couldn't swear to it, but I think so. I only caught a glimpse of him here, you know, looking down on him."

"Yes, of course. How long ago was it you saw Alice and this man together?"

"About a month, I suppose," replied Jennifer. "I couldn't honestly be sure, but I think I could make sure, if it were important, because it was when Ted—that's my fiancé—was in bed with flu, and I'd been to see him straight from the office."

"I'll let you know if it would help to be sure of the date," Roger said. "Did Alice ever speak of an *affaire*?"

"Well, yes and no—she didn't put anything into words, but I think she was in love at last," the girl answered, quietly.

"Can you be sure?"

"Well, I wouldn't have said so a few months ago, but since I—since I met my fiancé, I know the signs! Alice was always absurdly shy and timid, I used to get vexed with her sometimes. We were very good friends, really, although she didn't ever talk much about herself. She didn't have boy friends, didn't really like dancing, and I used to tell her that she wasn't giving herself a chance to live. Suddenly, everything changed. I was out most evenings, so I didn't know much about what she was doing—we've hardly had a chance to gossip lately, because I've spent every minute I could with Ted! But you could tell from the way she laughed, even the light in her eyes—I suppose that sounds absurd."

"Not a bit absurd," Roger assured her, and realised how

much he liked this girl. "It's a good thing to see. Didn't she tell you anything about this man?"

"Absolutely nothing," Jennifer assured him. "As a matter of fact, I wondered if that could be because he was married. I mean, *I* wanted to tell the world when I fell in love!"

"I can imagine," Roger said, and grinned. "Miss Ling, I'm going to get you to think about this statement, add anything that you recall, and dictate it to a shorthand writer who will come and see you later in the day. Are you going to be in?"

"I'm seeing Ted at half past one, he's calling for me."

"Perhaps he can help you remember," Roger said. "Will two o'clock be all right?"

"We were going out for a spin," Jennifer told him, "but I'm sure Ted wouldn't mind."

"Did he know Miss Murray?"

"Only slightly," the girl answered. "She did come in for coffee with us one night, but that was before she started going out a lot."

"Did you notice anything at all last night?"

"Nothing," Jennifer said firmly. "Nothing at all. I— well, shall we say that I was rather preoccupied?"

Roger laughed . . .

When he left her, he saw Fox, who was nearly finished in the bedroom, and had another word with the Divisional man in charge of the questioning in the street. Only two pieces of information had come in about the previous night; one man, arriving home late from his work as a waiter in a hotel, had noticed a man come along on a bicycle. This man had left his machine round the corner from Manville Street, along a stretch of Bell Street which was set aside for official parking. Another man had noticed an old car standing outside Number 24. Roger made mental notes of both of these and, a little after ten o'clock, went home.

Janet wasn't in the kitchen, and he felt a momentary pang of disappointment. Then he saw a note stuck on to a dish which held two sausages, two rashers of bacon and two eggs.

Sorry, dear, but if I don't do the shopping early all the vegetables will have been picked over. I'll be back about eleven. P.S. The boys have gone to the baths.

Roger shrugged off his disappointment, went to the larder and took out two cold sausages and a loaf of sliced bread, had a snack, washed it down with half a pint of milk, and went into the front room and telephoned the Yard. Nothing fresh had come in, but there was a message from Gill, at Anderson's shop; old Anderson was confined to his room with bronchitis and his son, Julian, was somewhere in the country, believed to be viewing some jewellery and silver plate at a mansion where the goods were to go under t!.c hammer early next week.

"So Julian isn't handy," Roger mused, and then asked: "Do you know when he's coming back?"

"Mr. Gill didn't leave any message, sir."

"Right. Tell him I'm going to see old Mr. Anderson first," Roger said. "Ask him to find out when the son is expected back at the shop."

"Very good, sir."

Roger went out, took the car out of the garage, and drove across town towards High Street, Kensington, thinking mostly about what the girl Ling had told him. Two men were already in the case, and he wished he could trace the middle-aged man, the lover-boy. His thoughts ranged over several possibilities; a jealous lover, for instance, or a married man who might be under some kind of pressure, who might possibly have been blackmailed. The quicker he had a look at the dead girl's bank balance, the better. Jennifer Ling was probably right in thinking the other girl being in love, but Alice Murray might also have been very pleased with herself if she were getting a handsome pay-off for not telling a wife about a husband's peccadillo. Roger called in at the Kensington branch of the MidPro Bank, the one named on her cheque books, and found it busy because it was Saturday morning; but the manager was eager to help the police.

When he heard of the murder, he looked really upset.

"I'm terribly sorry, terribly," he said. "I knew Miss Murray quite well, she used to come and bank money for Anderson's as well as herself. A most trustworthy and efficient young lady, I would have said. What a pity, what a pity! Her own account—well, she kept a balance of about two hundred pounds, and had nearly a thousand pounds in national savings certificates. As far as I know, she had no other securities, and certainly she hasn't been paying in any more money than usual—just her monthly cheque for a little over sixty pounds."

Certainly nothing here suggested that Alice Murray had been banking extra money; as certainly there was no obvious reason for thinking that a thief had killed her.

He went to the shop, where Gill, a tall and very thin man with a mournful expression, met him outside, and told him briefly what he could about the staff. There were four salesgirls, two salesmen, and a so-called 'manager', an elderly man named Parsons. The shop was double-fronted, one side filled with modern jewellery, the other with second-hand pieces, including some magnificent diamond rings.

"No sign of trouble here?" asked Roger.

"No, Handsome," Gill said, as if this was exactly the lack of results he had expected. "I checked the safes and the strongroom, and they're okay. There's a stock list in the little office at the back of the shop, where the girl worked, and old Anderson keeps another up in his flat. Nothing seems to be missing."

"Any word about son Julian?"

"Should be back this morning some time," Gill answered. "He had a crush on the girl all right—all the staff knew it."

"She respond at all?"

"The story is that she was too soft with him, she should have told him where to get off," answered Gill. "One of the girls says that she thinks that the real trouble was fear of losing a good job—she let Julian pet her a bit because of that."

"Julian a universal pawer?"

"Can't say the other girls have complained," answered Gill.

"What about the old man?"

"Very upset, I'd say," Gill answered. "Er—there is one thing I don't think you'll be very pleased about, Handsome. Would have prevented it if I could—" He broke off, obviously ill-at-ease.

"Let's have it," said Roger.

"Well, there are some newspaper chaps about, of course, and one of them overheard me saying that I wanted to talk to Julian, and when was he expected back. You know how these things get exaggerated in the press."

"Can't see that it will do any harm," Roger said, thoughtfully. "Who's with Anderson now?"

"An old housekeeper, who looks after both father and son," replied Gill.

Roger went upstairs to the flat, on his own. The elderly housekeeper was Scottish, tired-looking, and very harassed this morning, and she seemed worried about her employer. Roger heard the old man call out in a wheezy voice, and a minute later he stepped into the large bedroom, with its heavy, shiny mahogany furniture, figured tapestry curtains at the window, a little table at the foot of the bed with a typewriter on it, and the large double bed. Anderson was sitting up, a thin, bony-faced man with heavy-lidded eyes. He looked as if he were not just distressed, but grief-stricken; after the first few questions, he leaned back on high pillows, and said hoarsely:

"I simply can't imagine what my son will feel. He was so much in love with her. She was an obsession, a positive obsession."

"Was his love returned?" as if casually.

"No," answered Anderson quite frankly. "No, she had very little regard for him. She was a very kind person, but she had very little regard for him, although she wouldn't hurt his feelings for the world. There was a time when I thought there might be some hope for him, but lately—"

He broke off.

"What happened lately?" asked Roger, less casually.

The old man said in that hoarse voice while air bubbled in his chest: "I am a great believer in telling the truth to the police, Mr. West. I believe that you will find it out, whatever might be done to try to hide it, and I also believe that the truth cannot harm my son. Recently, Alice obviously fell in love with another man. Quite obviously so. Julian—Julian was terribly distressed by it, and he will be even more distressed by this awful news."

Even if he did it himself, Roger thought. He asked aloud: "Do you know the name of the man Miss Murray fell in love with, Mr. Anderson?"

"I do not, but my son might," answered the old man. "And if he can do anything to help you find this wicked murderer, I am sure he will."

Roger thought: I wonder if you're more cunning than honest. He didn't speak, just watched the man, whose blue-veined, scraggy hands were still on the white sheet, who looked as if he might die before this winter was out. He was old and shrewd and he was probably very, very clever. He might have talked of being honest and of making a statement which could implicate his son, simply to fasten attention on to Alice Murray's mysterious lover.

Then the housekeeper called out: "Mr. Julian!" and there was a flurry of footsteps, followed by heavier steps outside the door, which was thrust open.

Julian Anderson stepped inside.

7

MAN TO DISLIKE

IT would be easy to take a dislike to Julian Anderson on sight.

Roger studied the man, aware of the danger of prejudice and trying to push it away. It wasn't easy. Julian was in his early forties, nearly bald, with an unusually shiny, almost polished pate. Fleshiness disguised the fact that he was very like his father in features. He had a curiously powdered look, very smooth cheeks, a little chin framed by a roll of fat. Curiously, he was not really fat in the body, only plump. He wore a flowered waistcoat, beautifully coloured and smoothed down over his stomach, and a well-cut suit of a pale beige-coloured worsted, or some smooth material. A diamond ring flashed on his right hand; and his hands were plump and as pale as his face. Because of the fleshy face his eyes looked very small, but they were alert and intelligent, and much darker than his father's.

"What is happening?" he demanded. "What are all the men doing in the shop? Has there been a robbery?"

Roger glanced at the old man and saw how anxiously he was looking at him, Roger, not at his son.

"Father, tell me—" Julian began, and moved forward, hands spreading; and then he stopped, frowned, stared at Roger, and exclaimed: "You are Superintendent West!"

"Yes," Roger said.

"I thought so. I saw you in court on one occasion. But— only a very serious crime would bring you here. What is it?" He had a curiously mannered way of speaking, almost as if English were not his native tongue.

"My boy—" old Anderson began, and then broke off as if he could not bring himself to break the news.

"But what is it?" cried Julian.

Roger said: "Miss Alice Murray was cold-bloodedly murdered in her bed last night."

When his voice faded, there was silence except for the bubbly breathing of the old man; even that seemed subdued, as if he were trying to hold his breath. Roger kept reminding himself that he must not be prejudiced, that he must study this case with absolute detachment. Yet undoubtedly Julian looked as if he were putting on an act. He did it extremely well; perhaps too well. He stared at Roger, his eyes screwed up at first, his lips parted. Then his eyes opened wider, and he began to open his mouth slowly. He drew in a long, deep breath. The expression in his eyes changed, as one might expect it to change from shock. He began to raise his hands, which were clenched very tightly.

"No," he breathed. *"No."*

"My boy—" Anderson began again.

"No!" gasped Julian. "It isn't true, it can't be true. Not Alice, not—"

Roger said harshly: "A man with a key broke into her room, and strangled her while she lay in bed."

"Oh, God," gasped Julian. His right hand went to his collar, and he tugged at it as if it were choking him. He moved away from the door towards a chair, but did not sit down. "Oh, no," he breathed. "I can't believe—"

"Do you have a key to the flat?" demanded Roger.

Julian drew in a hissing breath.

"Please—" the old man began.

"Answer me. Do you have a key to Miss Murray's flat?"

Julian muttered: "I can't believe it. I just can't believe it." His face began to wrinkle, and he looked as if he were going to cry; if he did, it would be nauseating. Yet he also gave Roger the impression that he was really fighting hard for self-control. He lowered himself slowly on to the chair, putting one hand against a table, and pulled at his tie again.

"Do you or do you not have a key?" Roger rasped.

Julian stared at his father.

He said, still muttering: "Yes. Yes, I have a key. Oh, God, Alice! Who did this thing to you? Who did this awful thing?"

"Where is the key, Mr. Anderson?" Roger demanded icily.

"It—it is in my pocket."

"Did Miss Murray know that you had it?"

Julian didn't answer.

"Did she know, Mr. Anderson?"

"No," admitted Julian hoarsely, "she didn't know." He stared at his father, but gave the impression that he was not doing that consciously, that he was looking at some figment of his imagination; at the ghost of Alice Murray? He moistened his lips. "No, she didn't know."

"Why did you have it?"

"I—" Julian broke off again, letting the pronoun hang in the air.

"Mr. Anderson, the quicker you answer my questions the better it will be for you," Roger warned coldly. He wished that he had a sergeant here, taking notes; but if he sent for one it would break the present tension, and he wanted to hold that as taut as he could. "Why did you have the key?"

Anderson answered, hoarsely: "I loved her so much. I— I always believed that she would love me, that I would be able to win her round. I—I loved her so much. I couldn't think about anything else or anyone else. I only wanted to be with her. I dreamt of being in her flat when she came home, I used to try to make myself go there and wait for her, I thought if she knew how much I loved her she would submit to me. Oh, God," he breathed. "And she's dead."

"Were you at her flat last night?" Roger barked.

"I—"

"*Were you?*"

"No, no I wasn't!"

"*Were you at her flat last night?*"

"No," Julian whispered. "I swear I wasn't."

"When were you last there?"

"I—" Julian kept breaking off, but it was hard to say whether he was deliberately evasive, or whether he was genuinely suffering from shock.

"*When were you there?*" Each word was like a knife slash; and was meant to be.

Julian answered, dismally, despairingly: "I—I was in the street yesterday afternoon, yesterday evening rather. I hoped to meet her when she got home. She told me she was going straight there, she said that she was going to wash her hair, but—but she wouldn't let me take her home in the car. She did, sometimes, if I was waiting for her outside the shop, but last night she wouldn't let me. She said she wanted to do some shopping on the way. So I went to meet her as she reached her home but—she didn't come. I waited until seven o'clock, and she still didn't come, and—well, I've waited there before, and she's been back very late. Sometimes—sometimes I've actually gone into the house but I couldn't make myself go into her room. I thought—I thought she might misunderstand."

"Did you go in last night?"

"No. No, I couldn't wait out in the cold any longer, and I had some work to do."

Roger asked: "What work?"

"I was making up some invoices," Julian said, and then his face puckered up, and quite suddenly he started to cry. "Oh, God, not Alice, I can't bear it."

Roger wondered: "Can a man *act* like this?"

The tears in the man's eyes were genuine enough. He fought against crying aloud, and choked back his sobs. Pulling out a pure white handkerchief, he began to dab at his eyes. It was less crying than snivelling. He used his right hand, Roger noticed; nothing suggested that he was left-handed.

"Mr. West, can't you leave my son alone now?" asked old Anderson querulously. "He has suffered such a great shock, surely you can see that. Can't you let him rest?"

Roger said: "I'm afraid not, Mr. Anderson. I want him to come with me."

The old man exclaimed: "No!" He leaned forward from the bed, a scraggy hand stretched out, the sleeve of his pyjamas dragging back over the arm and baring it to the elbow; it was just brown, mottled skin and bone. "You're not going to arrest him."

"If Mr. Anderson can prove that he wasn't at Miss Murray's flat last night he has nothing to fear," Roger said formally. "I want him to come along with me to the morgue to identify the body."

"Oh, no," breathed the old man. "No, don't make him do that. Please don't make him do that."

"I understand that Miss Murray has no relatives in London," Roger said, "and identification by some person who knew her well is necessary. Have you any objection, Mr. Anderson?"

Julian looked at him vaguely. "Objection—objection to what?"

"I would like you to come and identify the body."

The man stared as if he did not really comprehend, and the shock had affected his mind and stultified it. The old man pleaded again, but there was neither vigour nor hope in his voice. At last Julian said: "I suppose—I suppose so." Roger took him downstairs, where a car was waiting with a sergeant at the wheel. He did not speak to Julian, but said to the sergeant:

"The morgue where the Murray girl's body is."

"Yes, sir."

Julian was staring straight ahead.

Roger had a feeling which seldom came to him these days; repugnance at what he was doing. One half of his mind was convinced that young Anderson was putting up an act, that all of this was being done in a tremendous effort to save himself from the consequences of the crime. The other, that this man was really grief stricken, and that he would be horrified and desolated by the sight of the dead girl.

The job had to be done.

The car pulled up outside the morgue next to the Chelsea police station. The sergeant jumped out. Moving automatically, Julian climbed out of the back of the car, and his legs seemed to be propelled by mechanism, not by any conscious effort of will. His cheeks had sagged. He kept blinking, rubbing his eyes, and sniffing.

The room where the body lay was cold. There were several empty stone slabs, and only one slab laden. A sheet covered the girl's body, which looked pathetically slender and small under the white shroud. There was no sound except Julian Anderson's sniffing. The morgue attendant was standing by the head of the girl. Roger went to the other side, with Julian close to him. He nodded to the man, who pulled back the sheet briskly, and Roger asked :

"Is that Alice Murray?"

Julian seemed to choke. "Yes—" he gasped. "Yes, that—" Then his legs bent beneath him, and he would have pitched on to the body had Roger not held him up.

* * *

"Funny how some of them can't take it," the morgue attendant said. "He the husband?"

"No," answered Roger.

A man could not make himself faint, he reasoned, and the suspect had been out dead cold. If Julian Anderson had murdered the girl in a fit of jealousy, or if his desire for her had reached an obsessional pitch, so that if he could not have her for himself he would prevent any other man from having her, collapse reaction now would be quite reasonable. The act of murder could shock a man so much that he would behave completely out of character. Awful repentance after it could explain such behaviour as this. Roger waited in the small office near the morgue, while Julian Anderson leaned back in a wooden armchair, coming round gradually, looking a dreadful colour.

The immediate question was whether to charge him.

If Roger did make a charge, there would be a chance of shocking this man into a confession, whereas if he were once given time to recover, his resistance might stiffen. He would undoubtedly get a good lawyer; his father would see to that. There was an odd fact to consider, too; neither of them had thought at once of sending for a lawyer, which might imply that they had in fact been taken by surprise. If Julian had anticipated a visit from the police, surely he would have decided well in advance what to do; and a man who had a sense of guilt would be ready to run to a lawyer.

That hadn't occurred to Julian, apparently.

His eyes were open now, and he took out his handkerchief and dabbed his damp forehead. The attendant came in with a cup of steaming coffee and a bowl of brown sugar. Roger stirred in two spoonfuls of sugar and handed the cup to Julian, who gulped, took it in trembling fingers and began to sip. He went on sipping mechanically, he did everything mechanically. When the cup was half empty, he put it down.

"Thank you," he said. "I won't have any more."

"Was it Miss Murray, Mr. Anderson?"

"Yes," Julian answered in the husky, whispering voice.

"Mr. Anderson, can you tell me where you were between twelve midnight last night, and two o'clock this morning?"

Julian didn't answer.

"Mr. Anderson, I know you have had a very severe shock, but it is essential that you answer my questions, for your own sake. Will you tell me where you were?"

"I—I was in my room," Julian replied. "Where else do you think I was? I was in my room."

There was a change in his manner; a kind of protective hardening.

Roger interpreted it as the transition from shock to fear. It showed in the glint in the little, buried eyes, in the way Julian's body seemed to hunch up, as if in self defence. He realised suddenly how vulnerable he was, perhaps realised that if he could not prove where he had been during those vital hours, there would be a case against him. He stared intently and intelligently into Roger's eyes, and there was no doubt at all that he was becoming more and more frightened.

"Can you prove that?" Roger asked.

Julian moistened his lips. "I—I went to bed at eleven o'clock, I didn't see anyone else until seven thirty when Jennie brought in my morning tea." He said all that almost gaspingly, as if he expected to be challenged, and he feared that it could be proved untrue.

"Very well, Mr. Anderson," Roger said, and stood up briskly. "I shall have to make a number of inquiries and check your statements. It would be in everyone's interest if you will co-operate in every way you can."

"What do you want me to do?" Julian Anderson asked, almost humbly.

"I would like you to come along to New Scotland Yard with me, make a statement confirming what you have already said, allow your clothes to be examined, and allow us to take scrapings from your finger-nails, a few hairs from your head, other things which may be helpful. At the moment you are under no compulsion to do these things. You would be, of course, if you were charged with the murder."

Now, the man really understood the danger he was in.

"I'll do anything you like," he said huskily, "but I didn't kill Alice."

* * *

He did everything that Fox asked him. Scrapings were taken from his shoes, dust from the turnups of his trousers, a few hairs were plucked from his head and nose and ears. He handed over the key of the girl's flat, which he admitted taking from her bag some weeks ago. His statement reiterated over and over again that he had been in love with Alice Murray, and that his unrequited love had almost driven him mad. And he talked of her meeting another man.

Roger studied the statement late that afternoon, and went along to the waiting-room to see the suspect again. Julian was looking more collected, but very pale.

"Did you ever see this other man?" Roger asked.

"No", answered Julian. "I used to follow Alice to try to find out who he was, but I didn't want her to know what I was doing, and she kept getting away from me."

"How do you know there was a man?"

"She changed," Julian answered, very slowly. "She—she used to be quite willing to let me take her home, and now and again she would come to the pictures with me. But about six months ago all that was over. I could tell she was in love with someone else, there was no doubt about that, and—and it made me desperate. I was afraid I would never win her."

If he were guilty, would he make such a statement as that?

And if he were guilty, surely he would have asked for a lawyer by now?

Did he realise how much the case against him would be weakened if the police could find this other man?

Roger knew that he would soon have to make up his mind whether to make a charge; this man had been here too long already. Roger asked him to wait for another ten minutes, and went up to his office, a small one overlooking the embankment. The lights of the traffic on Westminster Bridge showed up, and the lights of the bridge itself and of the embankment reflected on the swollen waters of the Thames. There had been flood warnings in the higher reaches, and a close watch was being kept on the river, but he gave that no thought as he thumbed through Julian's statement again, and looked through the reports from the Division and the Yard men who had worked at Manville Street as well as at Anderson's shop. The mass of statements and reports added nothing to what was already known. This other man seemed to exist, but only Jennifer Ling appeared to have seen him, and her description was never likely to help in evidence.

There was a tap at the door, and on his 'come in', Fox appeared. His bright eyes had an eager look, and Roger reminded himself that Fox might have ambitions to get away from his 'dry-cleaning'. He carried two plastic envelopes, and put them on the desk in front of Roger; this was plainly a moment of triumph.

"Well," Roger asked, and looked at several hairs inside one envelope, and two inside the other; they were short, grey and thin. "Whose?"

"Julian Anderson's."

"Positive?"

"Positive," asserted Fox. "Exhibit A, plucked from his head. Exhibit B, taken from the pillow of Alice Murray's bed. Exhibits C, D, E and F, on her clothes."

"Well, well," Roger said, and in that moment he felt as nearly certain as he could be that they had the right man in the unrequited lover. "Now all we want is to establish that he wasn't in his own room all last night."

"He wasn't," Fox said with satisfaction. "In that memo you asked me to send round the neighbourhood, I asked for any garage which might have supplied petrol. Found one on the Great West Road, sold him ten gallons about twelve fifteen last night. The description fits to a T, and they had the car number off pat—two K's and three 2's. So Julian A. was out and about! Going to charge him?"

"I think I will, now that I know he lied to me," Roger said, and ignored the fact that fear could make a man lie. Once a single lie was proved, it might be easier to make Julian admit to others. "Nice work, Charley, but do it my way in future, will you?"

"Your way?" Fox looked puzzled.

"If you want to add anything to an instruction, check with me first unless you can't find me. Then be absolutely sure it's the right thing to do."

"I won't forget," Fox said. "Thanks, Mr. West." He stood back as Roger stood up. "Like me to come along? My shorthand's good."

8

HOUSE FOR SALE

THE Sunday morning newspapers were delivered to John Payne's house about nine o'clock most Sundays, and the day after the family had slept so late he was up soon after eight o'clock. Gwen was still sleeping, although as he slid into his dressing-gown, he thought that she stirred. He went downstairs, made himself tea, and kept looking out of the front room window, in the hope that the delivery boy would be earlier than usual. At a quarter to nine, he heard Maurice whistling, and at ten to nine, Gwen called out:

"Maurice, go downstairs and see if your father's made tea."

"Okay, Mum!" Maurice came hustling.

The timing was bad, because the newspapers would come when he was drinking a cup of tea to keep Gwen company, Payne thought, but it would look odd if he stayed downstairs. He was on edge, although he felt sure that nothing would really worry him now; he was past the moment of crisis.

Maurice banged open the kitchen door.

"Hi, Pop! Mum says—"

"I heard her," Payne answered. "Put the kettle on, will you, and I'll take the tea up."

"Right-i-ho. Feel better this morning?"

"Much."

"You looked as if you'd spent a night on the tiles last night," Maurice said, and gave the kind of wink that he had learned from Gwen: he had Gwen's droll way of raising an eyebrow, and her broad humour; Hilda was the least humorous of the family, just a nice girl with a tendency to be affected whenever she wanted to create an impression.

74

"I'll give you night on the tiles," said Payne. "If you talk to me like that—"

There was a sound at the front door; the newspapers.

"—tan your hide," he finished. "You make that tea, I'll see what the latest sensation is."

"Never anything much in the papers on a Sunday," Maurice declared. "Wonder if they've arrested that chap Anderson yet, though." The murder had been a topic for eager family discussion last night.

There were two newspapers poking through the letter-box, and Payne hesitated before pulling them out. He felt almost as bad as he had once or twice yesterday; if this was going to keep on, it would make Gwen suspect some serious reason, and he must make sure that none of the family got that idea. Maurice's 'night on the tiles' worried him; would Gwen jump to the same kind of conclusion? Was it possible that she would suspect that they had all been drugged?

He pulled the newspapers out, with a sharp clack of sound, and opened the *Sunday Echo*. He clenched his teeth, for on the front page there was a photograph of Alice, and beneath it another, larger one, of Julian Anderson—a studio portrait taken some years ago.

The headline read:

EMPLOYER CHARGED WITH SECRETARY'S MURDER

After the first moment, when it seemed to leap into his throat, Payne's heart stopped pounding. He began to smile. After a few seconds, he felt completely free from any kind of fear, and in its place was a fierce kind of jubilation. Nothing could make him more secure than this. They must have a pretty strong case against Julian, and—it would take weeks, *months*, to get round to his trial! There was no need at all to worry, the heat was off for good.

As for Julian—

He had always thought him a stinker! It wouldn't do him any harm to stand trial. The police were bound to find themselves up against it eventually, he reasoned, when it really came to a trial they wouldn't be able to prove that an innocent man *had* committed the murder. So Julian wasn't really in danger. In any case, the question of proof would come much later. It wouldn't do the fat slug any harm to kick his heels in a remand cell, might even do him good.

Payne overcame his half-hearted scruples without much difficulty, and chuckled.

Maurice called: "Tea's made, Dad. You going to take it up, or am I?"

"I'll take it," Payne said, and hurried to the kitchen. "And here's the *Echo*." He tossed the boy the newspaper. "They charged Julian Anderson with Alice Murray's murder," he called out, so that everyone in the house could hear. "I never had much time for that nasty piece of work, but I'd have thought he'd stop at murder."

It would be the main topic of conversation for the next ten minutes, but after that there were likely to be only passing references. From this moment on, he could really begin to live. He'd show Gwen whether he could buy her mink and a new house! She would have to admit that he had not been bragging, he had just been waiting his opportunity.

He took it for granted that breaking into the shop and the strongroom would be easy; after all the care and thought he had given it, he could hardly go wrong. All his life, a facile optimism and overconfidence in himself had led him to failure, but he had never learned from his mistakes, had never learned how shallow his planning and his reasoning were. Now, excitement dulled any fear of failure, he was almost exhilarated as he watched Gwen while she read the report. She showed only a passing interest, and then turned the paper over in her hands.

"Let's start looking for somewhere better to live, pet," Payne suggested. "I've got a feeling in my bones that we'll be able to manage it soon. Any idea where you want to go?"

Hilda, coming along the passage, called : "Wouldn't it be lovely in the country, say out at Sunningdale, or—"

"I want to be within a threepenny bus ride of Piccadilly Circus," Gwen declared, flatly. "No one's going to get me to move out of this house to go any farther away. I feel buried even out here, and I can be in the West End in half an hour!"

"Better be near the West End for business, too," Payne agreed.

"I used to think that St. John's Wood would be a good place," Gwen went on, looking down the pictures of house advertisements, "but I've rather changed my mind. I think we ought to stay this side of London. Chelsea, say—I've always liked Chelsea." She wasn't looking at Payne, and did not see the way his lips tightened. "Somewhere between the river and King's Road, handy for the buses and nice for the evenings," Gwen went on. "It wouldn't be too far for Hilda, and Maurice's technical school would be within walking distance. Don't you think Chelsea would be the ideal place, Jack?"

She looked at him.

"Yes," he answered.

The moment he agreed he knew that it was a mistake; he should have been non-committal, or even found some quick reason for preferring some other part of London. The truth was, there was none better for his business, or for the children. Anyhow, Chelsea was a large borough, and he would soon forget how often he had been to Manville Street. The real reason for that spontaneous 'yes' was his fear of an argument with Gwen; he was frightened of her wanting to know why he cared so much, of being questioned about dislike of Chelsea. There was probably nothing suitable for them in Chelsea, anyway. It was like Gwen to start thinking *where*, already. She could never sit back and think about a thing, but had to be up and doing all the time. Well, why not let her? It would give her something to do, and houses were so difficult to find that it would probably take months before she came across anything suitable. In a month or so, he would almost have forgotten, wouldn't he?

And in a month or so, Julian Anderson would be up for trial.

Payne's almost ecstatic delight that someone else had been charged so that there was not the slightest risk of danger for him, became tinged with anxiety. If the police had not picked on Julian, the case would soon have died out of the newspapers; murders always did. Now there would be the police court hearing, then the trial, possibly a long one, and an appeal; it would be freshened in everyone's mind over a period of months, instead of dying quickly.

There was nothing *he* could do about it.

"You don't seem very interested, after all," Gwen said.

Payne laughed.

"I wasn't thinking of going out and getting a house tomorrow! I've these deals to put through, and they'll take a lot of negotiating before it's over. By the middle of March, say, we might start thinking seriously."

"You'd better be," Gwen said, and raised her voice. "Hilda! You can get the breakfast this morning, and bring mine up, I feel lovely and lazy. If Maurice wants any fried potatoes he can use up that mash we had the night before last, and mix in those sprouts. Tell him to use the pork dripping, that'll be tastier." She stopped shouting, and looked at Payne with the seductive smile which hadn't changed since they had first met. "Going to have your bath, or are you coming in with me?" she asked, wickedly.

*   *   *

Julian Anderson was formally charged with the murder of Alice Murray at a special Sunday morning court, held at half past ten. Roger and Fox gave evidence of arrest, Roger asked for a remand in custody, and a brisk, youthful looking solicitor who had been summoned after the arrest said that he had no questions to ask but wished to state that his client had a complete answer to the charge and, of course, pleaded not guilty. Julian Anderson seemed to be in a daze. The old man, out of his sick room for the first time for three weeks, looked as if he had not the strength to go back to it.

"I'll bet a fiver that Julian A. wishes to God he'd never done it, probably hates himself for it," Fox said. "I don't know how you feel, but I don't dislike the chap as much as I did. Something a bit pathetic about him."

"I know what you mean," said Roger.

He went from the West London Police Court to the Yard, and looked through reports, including a long list of articles found at the dead girl's flat on which there were finger-prints other than hers. There were cigarettes, some boxes of chocolates, books, magazines, some shiny books of matches. All of these had been taken to the Yard, and would be in *Fingerprints* now.

No one yet knew whose bicycle had been parked nearby last night, but Jennifer Ling had signed her statement and her boy friend, Ted-for-Edward Hardy, had added one of his own; he had heard and noticed nothing unusual.

Roger went up to *Fingerprints*, where a junior was on duty. There was the list of articles from the flat, with photographs of the prints found on them. Only one print found on each of two boxes of chocolates had not been identified as tradesman or neighbour.

"Same print on each box—a man's, larger than average," the trainee said.

"Hm, yes," grunted Roger. These might be taken as evidence that someone had bought the girl chocolates, but they might have been bought from a shop anywhere in the district, or farther afield. "No sign of this print on anything else?"

"No, sir."

"What about prints from the shop?"

"We've got specimens of all the staff's and old Mr. Anderson, sir. *And* the accused, of course."

"Any at the flat?"

"No, sir."

"Thanks," said Roger.

He saw the meticulous way in which each print had been photographed and registered, ready for the file; the Yard was nothing if not good at records.

He was back home in Chelsea in good time for the midday meal. The boys were out, Janet was in the kitchen, the pressure cooker was on. It was a surprisingly mild day for the middle of January, and the sun was shining on the misty film which covered the grass in the back garden, the three apple trees, and the few bushes which had been pruned close to the ground. Beyond the garden was another one like it, and beyond that a house which was let in three flats, and which badly needed a coat of paint.

"I'm really beginning to hate it here," Janet said, looking round from the pastry board, and then she made herself laugh. "Is that ungrateful, darling?"

"Ungrateful, what?" Roger had been thinking about Fox's change of feeling over the younger Anderson.

"After all, we *have* had some wonderful times here, even if you've forgotten," Janet said, half protestingly. "And the two boys *were* born here."

"Good lord!" Roger exclaimed. "So they were!" He leaned forward, pulled a small piece of uncooked pastry from a strip waiting to be placed across an apple pie crust, chewed it, and said: "We'll keep the children wherever we go, I'm all in favour of that. Sure you want to move?"

Janet turned to face him, a little flushed from the oven, a little wrinkled at the eyes and the corner of the mouth, but her eyes as bright and grey as ever. She wore an absurdly small, frilly apron, pouched rather high at the breast—a Christmas present from the boys.

"I am *quite* certain. Now don't start hedging."

"I was wondering whether you'd prefer to have this place really redecorated, top to bottom, and a lot of new furniture," Roger said, seriously. "All the front room and our bedroom for a start, and—"

"No," Janet answered, emphatically. "Twenty-one years in the same place is long enough, if we stay any longer we'll never want to go. What we need is a house large enough to turn into two flats when the children leave home, so that we can let one and add a bit to your pension."

"I don't get a pension for another fifteen years," Roger reminded her. "How are you going to support me before then?" He realised that flippancy was not suited to her mood, and went on hastily : "You're absolutely right, sweet. We'll start looking soon. But there's one condition."

Her eyes lit up.

"Roger, do you really mean it."

"I really mean it."

"I don't care what the condition is !"

"You probably will. Not a penny more than six thousand pounds, and not more than twenty minutes' drive away from the Yard."

"Oh, I don't want to change the *district*," Janet declared. Her eyes were glowing. "And if we can't get what we want for six thousand, we'll put up with what we've got. I know exactly what I want," she added, and although he was grinning at her she took no notice; but she had made him realise how deep was her longing to move from this house.

At five minutes to one, hot and flushed from a cycle ride, the boys came in. At five past, after a superficial wash, Richard's dark hair flattened with much water and brushing, and Scoopy's flat at the front but sticking up in a dozen ducks' tails at the back, they slid into their places at the table. Roger started to carve a leg of lamb. The boys were still flushed and eager, and it was Richard who said :

"I say, Mum, you know that house on the corner, where the people with that funny name live, Monty something."

"Montifiore," Scoopy supplied. "Can I help, Mum?"

"You can pull your table napkin up higher, I don't want to wash another shirt after it's been worn for five minutes. What about the house, Richard?"

"It's going to be sold," announced Richard, taking a

plate from Roger. "Thanks, Dad." He began to help himself to roast potatoes, quite oblivious of the way his mother was staring at him. "Micky Roberts told me, he lives next door, and his mother's always popping in and out of the Montforeys."

"*Mon—ti—fi—or—e*." Scoopy corrected, solemnly.

"For goodness sake let him say what he has to say," said Janet. "Go on, Fish."

"Well, apparently the *Mon—tee—fee—or—ees* are getting a bit old, she's over sixty-five apparently, and he's nearly seventy and they're going to retire and move down to the south coast, or Devon or somewhere, so the house will be for sale. Mrs. Roberts seems to think they'll have a difficult job selling it, though; they're going to ask some ridiculous sum, like eight or nine thousand pounds."

"Good lord!" gasped Scoopy. "He actually got it right!"

"Oh, that's ridiculous," Janet said, and her eyes were sparkling even more brightly. "They'll never get a penny more than six thousand five hundred. It's just—"

"Barefaced robbery," Roger put in quickly.

Scoopy's eyes widened, he stared first at Roger and then at Janet, and asked swiftly: "Here, what's on? We're not thinking of moving, are we? Why, the Montifiore's house must be the best in the district! Mum! Dad!"

"Could we, *possibly*?" pleaded Richard. They were both young again, children and not teenagers, with swift enthusiasm and glorious hopes.

"Well—" began Janet.

"We'd better tell them what we're thinking," Roger said, and thus began the longest lunch-time session they had had for months. Given their heads, the boys would have called on Mrs. Montifiore that very day. At last the telephone interrupted the excited discussion, and Roger got up to go into the front room, reflecting ruefully that the kitchen extension would never get done now. The boys began to help clear the table without prompting. Roger sat on the arm of an easy chair, feeling almost sure that this would be the Yard.

"West speaking."

"Good afternoon, sir." It was Fox, and his tone was subdued, immediately suggesting cause for alarm. "Sorry to worry you, but there's a bit of news that I think you ought to know right away."

"Let's have it."

"Old Mr. Anderson collapsed just before lunch, and died before they got the doctor," Fox reported. "Poor show, isn't it?"

Roger said, slowly and heavily: "Very. Thanks for calling." He hesitated, and then went on: "Does Julian Anderson know?"

"No, sir." Fox's voice quickened. "That's a job for Keston, his solicitor surely."

"Is it?" asked Roger. "I think I'll go along to Brixton." It wasn't going to be a pleasant task, or one he would be proud of, but if he gave Julian this news the man would surely be in the very depths of despair, and might possibly be shocked into telling the truth.

*   *   *

Julian Anderson sat very still on the wooden chair in the remand cell. He had not moved since Roger had come in. He had not flinched when he had been told about his father, and yet Roger had the impression that the news struck deep. The silence lasted for a long time, before Julian said, in his slow, hurt voice:

"Thank you for coming, Mr. West. I appreciate your thoughtfulness, it would have been easy to leave it to someone else. But Mr. West—this is two lives the murderer is responsible for. He really killed my father." The little porcine eyes were strangely steady as he went on: "You won't mind me saying that I like you, Mr. West. That may sound peculiar, but although we're on different sides you've always been very considerate. You've got your job to do, and if I'm the innocent victim of circumstances I can't blame you. I can see exactly how your mind works, and how black it looks against me. But as true as I'm standing here, I did not murder Alice. I did go into the hall, I lied to you about that because I was frightened, but I was not in her room on Friday night. I left, and went for a long drive, I was so miserable, and speed helps me a little. But I did not kill Alice. Someone else committed that crime, and the same person is responsible for the death of my father. It may sound rather sentimental to you, Mr. West, but they were the only two people for whom I really cared. That is the simple truth. If I were outside, free to do what I liked, I would dedicate my life to finding the murderer. I mean that in deadly earnest—I would dedicate my life to the task."

He paused again, as if he realised just how telling this quiet statement of his case was; how cunningly he was putting doubt into Roger's mind. "If the law does find me guilty, Mr. West, it will be a mistake. I understand that I cannot be hanged, as the law now stands, but I can lose my liberty for life. I want you to believe me when I say that I would sacrifice that, readily, if I could only make sure of finding the murderer.

"Whether I am found guilty or innocent, Mr. West, I would like to feel that you were still looking for the killer. Will you do that?"

*   *   *

Was he almost fiendishly clever; or was there the simplicity of truth in what he said?

Roger was uneasily preoccupied by this question as he drove back to Chelsea, and glad that the boys had gone out with some friends. Janet was content with the Sunday afternoon television and her dreams, and Roger was able to sit back and let everything about the Murray girl's murder pass through his mind. As if they realised that he was pondering over the case, the boys were in a quiet mood when they got back, and Janet did not harass him with questions until they were getting ready for bed. Then she asked shrewdly:

"Aren't you sure about Julian Anderson?"

"I'm going to spend tomorrow combing every bit of evidence with Gill and Fox, and then take the case to Hardy," Roger said. Hardy was the then Assistant Commissioner for Crime. "If I've slipped up on this, the quicker it's put right the better."

Next morning, he was still uneasy, almost to a point of being worried; Anderson's earnest simplicity seemed to haunt him. He found Fox and his own chief *aide*, Detective Inspector Cope, huddled together over his desk. Cope was a big, burly man who had broken an ankle some months before and was just getting about again; he still needed a stick. Fox looked as if he had just come out of the forests.

"What have we got?" demanded Roger.

"The last nail for Anderson's coffin," Fox said, without jubilation. "We've got everything, now. Remember that Jennifer Ling's fiancé said he saw a Jaguar pass in Bell Street?"

"Yes."

"We've had the number checked: it was Anderson's car. And we've had a bit of luck from a neighbour who was out yesterday and Saturday. Got in about half past eleven on Saturday night, he says, and saw Julian A. actually going into Number 24. So he's lying hard to save himself."

Roger didn't say that Julian had already admitted that, and didn't speak, until Fox said with unexpected feeling:

"Poor devil."

"I'd poor devil him," Cope said. "We ought to wave flags because we've got him so quick."

9

NEED FOR SPEED

THE case against Julian Anderson seemed as tight as it could be. The Assistant Commissioner and the Public Prosecutor's office agreed. For safety's sake, another eight-day remand in custody was asked for, but after that it would almost certainly be plain sailing, with a straight committal for trial at the Old Bailey. From Roger's knowledge of the Assize calendar, it would be March before the trial, and it might possibly wait over until May.

Julian was allowed to leave Brixton on the Tuesday, for his father's funeral. Tearful Jennie and two elderly friends of the old man were there, as well as a sprinkling of business acquaintances, and a representative from the bank—the manager to whom Roger had spoken. And, of course, there was a hoard of newspaper men. Julian, white and drawn, stood up to the strain well. The two policemen, and two prison officers with him did not crowd him too much, and although every precaution was taken to make sure that he made no attempt to escape, the whole function went off without sensation. The evening newspapers gave it headlines:

TRAGIC FIGURE AT GRAVESIDE

That was about right, Roger thought.

When he got back to the Yard, there was a buzz of excitement over an escape from Dartmoor, and a spasm of action over a post-office van hold-up in the West End. A man the Yard had been looking for during the past three weeks was picked up not five minutes walk from his home, and a harassed and alarmed bank official reported that he had discovered some remarkable forgeries of one pound notes;

there would be upheaval over that if the notes had been in circulation for long, and it promised to become a major inquiry.

The case against Julian Anderson became a matter of routine, now mostly handled by the P.P.'s office. It stopped nagging at Roger, because of that last piece of straightforward evidence. There was virtually no doubt that the jury would bring in a guilty verdict.

Roger did hear, three weeks later, that Julian was putting the family business on the market. That looked like a covert confession of guilt, or at least acceptance of the fact that he would not be free to run the business. The plump man with the fat face, whom it was easy to dislike on sight, became more and more a tragic figure.

*　　*　　*

The fact that Anderson & Son was on the market became generally known in the jewellery trade just three weeks after Julian's arrest, and John Payne heard about it when he called on a firm of wholesale jewellers and gold- and silversmiths in the Chancery Lane area. A little old man with owlish eyes and a permanently husky voice stood in his shirt sleeves behind an overheated shop, and said :

"I expect you've heard, Mr. Payne, about what is happening at your old place of business."

"What's new, Mr. Benoni?" asked Payne, opening the case in which he had a few sets of cheap jewellery, and several small collections of antique jewellery which he had picked up at a sale three weeks ago. He was visiting all the main wholesalers, knowing that some would buy without asking too many questions, for he might possibly need to sell a great deal of the Anderson stock in a hurry. He had also visited several of his retail customers, telling them that he had taken over two or three small shops in the provinces, and that he would have a much larger selection to offer within the next few weeks. When eventually he showed them jewels taken from the Anderson stock, no one would be surprised; the vital thing was to make sure that he did nothing to attract attention.

"So you haven't heard," little old Benoni said. "You spend too much time out of London, Mr. Payne. London is the place for keeping your ear to the ground. It is up for sale."

Payne exclaimed : *"What?"* and positively gaped at the man.

"Well, well, is that so surprising?" Benoni asked. "What can Julian do there now? And old Clayton, was he any use even in your day? What a pity it is that you don't work there now, Mr. Payne, you might have been given a chance to manage the business."

Payne said, with a jerky laugh : "I'm doing a lot better on my own than I ever was there. I couldn't stay in all day, anyhow—give me a life on the open road! Are you sure about this, Mr. Benoni?"

"Oh, yes," the old man assured him. "I was in the silver vaults this morning, and Clayton was at the Anderson vault. He is worried in case the new owners find out what a useless old man he is!"

"Why don't *you* buy it?" asked Payne.

"Me? What would I be doing with a retail business, my boy? Now there is something I want to tell you. I have a big market, in America, a very big market, for Regency jewellery. I can sell all antique jewellery there but just now the Regency market is very big for America. That is what I wanted to say to you—remember me, when you go round to see these different collections."

Payne said : "I won't forget you, Mr. Benoni."

"That's good, that's good," the old man said. "I am not telling a lie, Mr. Payne, when I say that I could sell a hundred thousand pounds worth of Regency jewellery—and Louis XVI, if it comes to that. It's a big market, and I will get a good price, so I could pass on a good price, couldn't I? You will give me the first offer, Mr. Payne, won't you?"

"You'll get the first offer," Payne assured him.

He left the shop and went straight across the road to a snack bar where he bought a cup of tea and a doughnut, and took them to a table in the window. He watched the passers-by, the rumbling buses, the speeding taxis, but hardly realised they were there. His heart was racing with excitement fired by new anxiety. If the Anderson business was to change hands, valuers would soon be going down into the strongroom, and checking over the stock. There might soon be new, complete stock lists available, so that practically everything at Andersons would be easily identified. No one in the trade would buy the business without a valuation, and the physical task might take several weeks. It was even possible that there would be special precautions at the strongroom; Julian Anderson had grown into the habit of doing whatever his father wished, but anyone with half-an-eye would know that the old strongroom and the old-fashioned safes could be opened almost as easily as a tin can.

That was the cause for anxiety.

Old Benoni was the cause of excitement. His offer to buy practically anything was precisely what he, Payne, needed. Manna from heaven. Benoni didn't talk out of the back of his neck, either; the market was there. He had betrayed the fact that he had access to it, but not exclusive right to sell to it, when he had asked for a first offer of anything that Payne picked up. This meant that there was a big American buyer in London, on the look-out for exactly the kind of jewellery that Anderson's specialised in. Payne knew it so well. There were stacks of old 'junk' in the strongroom, some of which hadn't been dusted for years, kept by old Anderson as a kind of safety valve; Anderson had always been a great believer in having a big stock and a small bank account. Today's stock might double its cash value in ten years, he had reasoned, and cash would almost certainly lose its value.

"I've got to get there soon," Payne told himself, and fought down the excitement. He drank the lukewarm tea, and added: "I've got to do it tonight or tomorrow."

He was almost sick with excitement.

There was no new problem, of course; he knew exactly what he had to do, exactly how to get into Anderson's and out again. From the conception of this plot, he had known that there was only one serious problem: how to get *enough* of the stock away. Jewellery weighed heavy. He would take it out of its cases, and wrap it in cotton wool, but there was enough at Anderson's to fill a dozen trunks. The problem had always been one of selection: what would pay him best? Now, it looked as if he knew.

Words dazzled him. An old man's voice thrilled him. *A hundred thousand pounds worth.*

"Take it easy," Payne advised himself anxiously. "Don't be greedy."

Gwen didn't want a fortune, and the safe thing would be to take just enough to set him up properly in business, and to buy that new house. Say, thirty thousand pounds. But if it were as easy to get a hundred thousand as thirty thousand, why not? He could discount old Benoni's figure, of course— take twenty-five per cent off. But even then, seventy-five thousand pounds was worth thinking about, and this way it would be through the normal channels, it wouldn't be 'hot' in the accepted sense of the word. Alice had told him exactly where the records were kept at Anderson's shop; the old fool had just muddled on, and Julian hadn't been any better. Once the records were destroyed no one would really know how much had been stolen.

Payne snorted with laughter, it was so perfect.

He made three more calls that afternoon, and each time was told of the fact that Anderson's was on the market. By casual questioning, too, Payne made sure that old Jennie was still at the flat, and there had been no other changes as far as was known. Locks and keys were the safeguard. His mind was racing furiously as he talked and listened. He certainly had little time to lose, but the fact that the crisis compelled him to act quickly was a stimulant, and he checked over his preparations with great care. He would get into the

hallway of the flat, the door of which had the window between it and the shop door. The flat door opened on to the
narrow hall and an equally narrow staircase. A door led from
this passage into the shop, and also to the door of the strongroom. If the flat door from the street was bolted as well as
locked, he would go round to the back, where there was another entrance to the passage. The shops in the street were
served from a road which ran along the back, and among
them was an off-licence and a pub, which were open until
half past ten, so there was risk of being seen. But he could
take a car or a van right to the back door.

If he rigged up a false number plate on his car, and that
would be easy, he could have one in the boot against emergency; it could be done easily, too.

The familiar thumping sensation at Payne's chest was almost painful; he could hardly wait.

He had to get in about eight o'clock in the evening, he
reasoned, he had always known that. If he went much later
he would be too conspicuous, for after eleven o'clock, the
police often sneaked up at the back of the pub and the off-
licence to find out if sales were being made out of hours.
So he had to be finished by ten thirty. The task itself would
take very little time; once inside it was simply a question
of opening doors and filling up the suitcases.

He had four, in which he kept his larger samples. When
he had bought them, months ago, he had made sure that
they were lightweight but very strong. Each was medium-
sized, because he had checked and made sure that a larger
case would be too heavy. Two of medium size should win
him about twenty thousand pounds worth of jewellery each,
because he would make his first selection among the better
quality goods; a second trip would be worth about half as
much.

He had planned two trips; now he began to think of the
possibility of a third. Each should take about twenty minutes, no more. If he had his car, or hired a van for the
occasion, he could have it close to the back door of the shop,

and be able to load straight away. He could have three loads out in an hour.

Of course there *were* risks, but he believed that he had reduced them to an absolute minimum. Even the fact that he had to operate more quickly than he had expected reduced one—the possibility that the waiting would begin to wear at his nerves.

Tomorrow?

Or tonight?

He could tell Gwen that he had a special offer of goods to inspect—that would be the simple truth. Suddenly, he burst out laughing. That was right : strike while the iron was hot! He had the suitcases, he had his car, he only needed false number plates to fit over the genuine ones, and the risk would be almost negligible once he got inside the premises.

It couldn't fail.

*   *   *

It looked as if the fates were working with him, Payne thought exultantly, for rain began to fall about half past six that evening, and rain kept people in, while those who braved it did not look about them when they were out. He had telephoned Gwen, who had accepted the news without protest; she seldom protested, partly because he was not often out in the evening; she was always sure that whenever he was it was for a good reason.

He selected a car park not far from Anderson's shop, to fix the false number plates, and had no difficulty. It was a little before eight o'clock when he turned off Kensington High Street into the side turning and the service road. Very little traffic was about; people were in the restaurants, in pictures and theatres or watching their television, for this was the dead hour of the evening. He drove carefully past the back of the well-lit public house and the off-licence, as carefully past a shoe shop and a little café, which was open. Then he reached the yard at the back of Anderson's.

The whole place was in darkness.

"It's just right," he told himself aloud. "Everything's going right."

He left the car and went round to the front to try the door; he was not really surprised to find it was bolted. Just as well! He hurried round to the back again, and thrust the key into the back door. He felt it turn, and pushed the door. It hardly moved.

God!

Why was it bolted back and front? It had never been in the old days until late at night, when everyone was in bed. It—

God!

Old Anderson was dead, Julian was in prison awaiting trial, so old Jennie lived here alone, scared out of her wits. She would see to the bolts. He ought to have realised that the place would be locked and bolted more securely than he had known it, but hadn't given that a thought.

The silly old bitch!

It did not occur to him to blame himself, and he fumed at old Jennie as he stood with the rain hissing and splashing behind him, the sound of occasional cars in the street beyond the houses.

He couldn't get in without breaking a window, and that meant making a noise.

He knew the old alarm system and how to get past it without attracting attention, but at last he woke up to the fact that the police or the trustees of old Anderson's estate might have put in a new one. That was another thing he had overlooked; there would *be* trustees, the bank—the MidPro Bank with its branch just along the street. Banks always took excessive precautions. Other possible obstacles seemed to rise up in his mind. The people he had questioned might have been guessing, it was even possible that most of the stock had been taken away. Was there a night-watchman? Was the shop being kept under observation?

Sweating, he moved away from the door. No one appeared to be about, it was raining more heavily, and there was a shed with a tin roof on which the rain hissed and rattled. He reached the High Street. No one appeared for a full half minute, then several cars came along, lights shimmering on the wet road, and several pedestrians hurried. He saw nothing to suggest that the shop was being kept under surveillance, and when he came to think about it dispassionately, he realised that there was no reason why it should be : no one had been murdered *here*.

So that he could see into the doorways of the nearby shops on the same side of the road as Anderson's, Payne crossed over. Then he saw the light at the third and top floor window, and realised Jennie was there, or else someone was in Jennie's old room. He began to feel better. Why imagine that it would be anyone else? The old crow had lived there for fifty years, where else would she go? He could picture her sitting up in her bed-sitting-room, with the television. The old man had bought her a twelve-inch television several years ago, and she sat huddled over its wriggly picture evening after evening. Payne had been there only now and again when he had been employed by Anderson, always with a message for the old woman.

If she was in, she could open the door, couldn't she?

Would she?

Why shouldn't she? Payne reminded himself that there had been no violence here, and that the shop was locked and bolted back and front, there was no reason why Jennie should expect trouble, she would just be nervous.

Then an idea darted into Payne's mind : why not telephone her, why not say he wanted to see her? He was an old employee, she surely wouldn't suspect him. He could say that he had heard that the shop was for sale, and he believed he had a buyer. He could even say that he had done so well that he was in the market for it himself ! Of course, she would see him. That was the whole point—she would let him in because she knew and trusted him.

Of course, he couldn't let her live, but—

What good did an old woman like that do herself or anyone else?

He walked quickly through the teeming rain towards a
telephone kiosk, and swore beneath his breath as his wet
cuffs and wet coat made it difficult to get out the coppers
he needed. But soon the number was ringing, and before
long old Jennie answered.

10

COINCIDENCE?

"COME to the back door," Jennie had said in her broad Scots, "and I'll meet ye there."

Payne waited for her.

It was five minutes since he had put down the receiver, and he could not understand why she had been so long. Because the raid had started badly, his mind was full of forebodings, and he was obsessed by them just as he had been by the advantages. Could Jennie possibly suspect his purpose? Had she anyone else with her? He had not asked, hoping to make sure that her suspicions weren't aroused. Had she even telephoned the police?

Why the devil should she?

Payne began to shiver, only partly because of the cold. Then a car turned into the service road, its headlights on and dipped, and in a moment of awful fear he thought that this might be a police car. *Could she have sent for them?* The car came on, slowly. He could see the silvery streaks which the heavy rain made against the headlamps. He could just make out the outline of the driver and a passenger, a man and a woman. The police wouldn't come in courting couples, he told himself fiercely. The car came on, and passed very slowly; it stopped three or four shops along, out of sight. He heard the car door open, and then close with a bang; he thought he heard footsteps, but soon silence told him that someone had gone into one of the other shops.

He heard a creak behind him, and spun round. The door bolts were being drawn back. He waited tensely until the door opened a foot, and saw Jennie outlined against the dim light of the back staircase. He saw no one else. She wore a black shawl, and her grey hair was frizzy and wispy against the light A squall of rain blew in, and she said testily :

"Ma goodness me, man, come in oot of the rain." She stood aside, and Payne went in, his wet raincoat brushing against her. "Man, ye'll catch your death," she said, in the half querulous, half complaining tone that she had often used with old Anderson. "Why don't ye take your coat and hat off and leave them doon here?"

"Yes, I will," said Payne. "Nice to see you again, Jennie."

"I don't know what ye've come for," she said, more shrilly than before. "I'm not saying there's any information I can give ye, Mr. Payne. Tae think ye've made enough money to consider buying Mr. Anderson's own business!" There was a note of admiration in her voice, and Payne thought that he detected something else, a kind of craftiness. "I'd like tae feel it was owned by someone I knew," she went on. "I'm too old a body to be thrown out to find somewhere else to live."

So that was it! The old crone was thinking of her future, and eager to find out what he had in mind. It was difficult not to laugh. She walked slowly up the stairs, one step at a time; she had an arthritic hip, he knew, and he could hear it creaking with every step she took. Life was really a burden to her, and whoever took over the premises would not want an old cripple on their hands.

Payne said : "Don't you get nervous, living here by yourself, Jennie?"

"Och, what is there for an old body like me to be nairvous aboot?" she asked, and gave a cackle of laughter. "No one would want anything of me, would they now?" She was halfway up the first flight of stairs, and for the first time, Payne heard the television voices. "Is it for yourself you're thinking of buying the business or are you acting for a thaird party?"

Payne said : "It's for myself."

He was wondering : How shall I do it?

He remembered how he had killed Alice, how easy it had

been, how quick. It would be even easier with Jennie, because she was older and would not be able to put up any kind of fight. He had to shift that shawl, which would prevent him from getting a tight grip on her neck, but the ends might be pinned together under her chin, he couldn't remember whether that was her custom or not. They reached the first landing, and Jennie stopped, grunting, and turned to look at him.

The shawl was not fastened; all he need do was to whip it off when she turned her back on him again.

The television voices sounded louder.

Jennie went on towards the next, narrower flight of stairs, and started up them slowly; she was breathing more heavily, and did not attempt to talk.

They were halfway up the stairs when Payne snatched a corner of the shawl away, and bared her scraggy neck.

*　　*　　*

He could not stand the television voices.

He stepped over old Jennie's body, and went up to her room. An electric fire was burning, both bars on, and the room was much hotter than she would ever have dared to keep it in Anderson's days. The television was on too loud. The picture was blurred a little, but it showed a girl answering a question in some quiz programme. The girl reminded Payne of Alice Murray. He stretched out his gloved hand and turned the set off; the ensuing silence seemed to hum about his ears. He saw that Jennie had put out a whisky bottle, so she had been going to do the honours. He eyed the bottle longingly, and then promised himself aloud :

"Later."

He went downstairs, climbed over the motionless body again, but when he reached the door leading to the shop and the strongroom he had forgotten old Jennie. It was going to be easy, all the difficulties were over. The keys turned smoothly, and the first door opened. Excitement held him taut for a few seconds, but he soon began to thaw. The strongroom door was as straightforward as he had hoped, because of the key which he owed to Alice.

The safes were easy to open with the old keys, too, and were crammed from top to bottom with all he had hoped to find; they had accumulated a huge stock. The only problem was to grade it, most of it was in a hopeless jumble. He told himself that this was due to Clayton's inefficiency; with both the Andersons away, the manager was carrying on by himself, and he had always been a muddler.

Silly old fool.

Then Payne opened a safe which was in apple-pie order, and recognised the hand ˋof Julian. Soon he realised that this was the valuable jewellery he had really come to find.

*   *   *

The job was over in an hour and twenty-five minutes from the time Payne had first parked the car at the back. He had filled the cases, and had destroyed the stock lists in the strongroom and in the little office—and no one was ever likely to be surprised, because everything else was in such confusion. Probably no one would ever be sure that there had been a stock list, and old Clayton would be blamed for losing it, anyhow.

The whole operation went just as smoothly as he had planned.

He closed and locked the back door, and drove back to Richmond Hill Road. He took out his 'sample cases' and carried them one at a time to the workshop, bent down and cleared away the oddments which covered the hiding-places, and put the stolen goods in there. He felt as sure as it was humanly possible to be that no one would dream of looking there—unless the police had some reason to suspect him.

Why should they?

And even if they did, even if they ever found some of the jewellery, why should they think it was stolen? It was as near certain as could be that the records at Anderson's place were poorly kept. The insurance cover was for overall value, seldom for specific items, and he knew that no single piece he had taken was worth more than a hundred pounds or so. Very few would have to be described for insurance purposes.

Within a day or two he could start selling to Benoni!

Now, he needed that drink.

It was still raining, and the wind was gusty and unpleasant. He went in by the back door, switched on the bright light of the kitchen, heard the television set going, hung his wet coat behind the back door to drain off, kicked off his wet shoes, and went on his stockinged feet towards the living-room. He heard Gwen say:

"Oh, why don't you turn the rubbish off, and read a book or something?"

"It's jolly good, Mum," Maurice protested.

He ought to be in bed, of course, but Payne was in no mood to act the heavy father. He banged a door, and strode into the living-room. Maurice jumped up from his chair, voice eager in spite of shadows beneath his eyes.

"Hallo, Dad! Mum said I could just stay up and see this Western."

"And I've regretted it ever since," declared Gwen. "Did you get very wet, Jack?"

"Not too bad, but I'd better change my trousers," Payne said, then clapped his hands together with a report which drowned the shots coming from the screen. He had to talk, he had to boast, he had to have their praise. "Turn that off, chaps, and gather around! Maurice, pour me out a whisky, and be sparing with the soda!" He saw the excitement in their eyes, Gwen's especially, and went on with his arms spread out as if he were exhorting a crowd. "Believe it or not, I have just completed the biggest deal of my life!" As he said that, it was the most natural thing to look excited, to put the right note into his voice; and this was exactly what Gwen wanted to believe. He had not felt so good for years for both wife and son were already eager and excited. "I've been nursing the deal for weeks, and wasn't sure it would come off," he went on. "There was an old shop in Watford with a lot of stock, mostly Regency jewellery and some French baubles, and I knew that there was a big American buyer coming over from New York for that kind of junk. So I got an option on the goods at a give-away price, the chap who owned them didn't know the value of what he'd got! I paid him a fair price though, young Maurice, even though business is business. He wouldn't have got any better from anywhere else, and I happened to have this inside knowledge. Anyhow, the Yank's in England, he's buying big, and without putting a penny of our savings down, I can make enough for the deposit on that new house!"

He saw radiance spring into Gwen's eyes.

Maurice brought him the whisky and soda, but before handing it to him slapped him on the back.

"Marvellous, Pop! I always knew you'd make it."

"It's *wonderful!*" Hilda said.

"So you've really pulled it off," Gwen said, and her quiet tone was a tribute in itself.

"I've pulled it off, and there's plenty more of the same," Payne said gloatingly, and downed his drink.

From now on, it was simply a matter of filling in the details, and none of the family was ever likely to question him closely about the deal. The whole thing was working out like a perfectly planned operation should.

When undressing that night he wondered when the police would find the old woman's body.

*   *   *

Roger West stepped into his office the next day, a little after eight o'clock, early because there had been a bank robbery during the night and he had to check some of the fingerprints found at the scene of it. He worked solidly on the case until half past nine, eased off, ran through all the other reports on his desk, then glanced across at Cope, who was looking harassed and restless; before long he would tire of the indoor work, bad ankle or not.

"How about a cuppa, Jim?" Roger asked. "Shall we send for one?"

"Mind if I hobble down and get one at the canteen?" asked Cope. "I don't mind your ugly dial, but sitting cooped up in one place gets on my wick. Don't think I can stand it much longer."

"What's the latest report on the ankle?"

"They hope to take the plaster off next week," Cope answered. "Shall I send a cup up to you?"

"No—I'll go down when you're back," Roger said. "What makes you think having an ankle in plaster is the only reason to hate being anchored to a desk?" He won a grin from Cope, and the burly man was in a better frame of mind when he went out. It was a pity about Cope; a Yard doctor had said that he doubted whether the ankle would ever stand up to heavy work again, and Cope had been one of the most active of men.

Roger was looking through the bank break details, so far as he yet had them, when the telephone bell rang, and Hardy, the Assistant Commissioner, said :

"Can you come and see me, Handsome?"

'Can you?' was rhetorical.

"Right away," Roger said. He rang off, called the exchange to put his calls through to Hardy's office, and went out briskly. Charley Fox was coming out of a sergeants' office.

"Dry-cleaned that bank properly?" Roger demanded.

"I will say one thing about banks, they keep the spit and polish on," Fox retorted. "I'll have a report ready by eleven o'clock. Can't say I expect much for you."

"Do the best you can," Roger urged. He saw Fox lug the bag of a vacuum cleaner into the small room where he did most of the examination of the proceeds of his cleaning, then went along to Hardy's office. Hardy was another heavily built man, rather quiet and sometimes aloof, who had come up from the ranks. He was not popular with everyone, but Roger had never had a serious clash with him, and rather liked what he knew of the man.

"Come in, Handsome," Hardy said. He had on a new, well cut navy blue suit. His grey hair had just been cut very short and he had a fresh, scrubbed look. Roger thought : The Commissioner's Conference, of course. It was a morning to pay deference. "Good morning, sir."

"Got a funny one for you," Hardy said. "Don't remind me that you've got enough on your plate already, I know it. But if it's necessary, hand that bank job over to Soames or McLiesh." He paused, picking up a slip of memo paper, and Roger knew that whatever job he had in mind must be an important one; the Yard disliked switching its senior officers from one case to another. "Remember that old woman at Anderson's flat?"

Roger's eyes narrowed.

"Yes. Jennie Campbell."

"That's right. Found on the stairs this morning—dead."

"Not *strangled*."

"Strangled."

"Good God!"

"Funny turn up for the book, isn't it?" Hardy remarked. "Could be coincidence, of course."

Roger didn't speak, but his mind was already beginning to race.

"Don't you think so?" Hardy asked.

"Coincidence? Wouldn't like to rule it out, but I want to see that body, quick," Roger said. "Any of our chaps over there yet?"

"No, only the Divisional people," Hardy replied. "I told them you would be coming over. I suppose you want Fox," he added, with one of those quick flashes of understanding which made him easy to work with. "Better take him."

"Thanks," Roger said gratefully. "I really ought to have the same team as with Alice Murray."

"Prise 'em away from other jobs if you can."

"Thanks," said Roger again. "Any other details?"

"Thomas of the Division called me when you were over at the bank," Hardy replied. "Just reported that he'd had a call from the shop, and he thought we ought to know pretty quick. Trying to wash his hands of this one, of course."

"Suits us, sir," said Roger.

There were mornings when Hardy would say 'forget the sir'; this morning it bolstered up his ego. In a few minutes he would be with the other bigwigs, feeling rather out of place. Roger went out, striding, and looked into Fox's cubby hole. Fox was peering at a little pile of dust which had been shaken out of the bag of the vacuum cleaner on to a sheet of white cardboard. He had a pair of eyebrow tweezers in his hand, and kept picking out small objects.

Roger let the door bang.

"That's right, that's right, let's have an Atlantic gale in here so we can make a proper dust storm," Fox said irritably. "Why the hell—oh." He looked round. "Sorry, sir!" The change in his expression was comical.

"I'm the one to be sorry," Roger said, grinning. "Cover that up with a windproof bag, will you? I've got some real work for you."

"Dunno that I like the sound of that," Fox said. "What is it?"

Roger told him.

"Well, you never know, do you?" said Fox, heavily. He shook out a large polythene bag, and Roger held it open while Fox slid the sheet of cardboard with the pile of dust into it, then folded the end of the bag and sealed it; Fox was one of the most thorough men at the Yard. "I'll go and get the vacuum cleaners," he added. "Shall I meet you downstairs?"

"How long will you be?"

"Five minutes."

"Downstairs, then."

Roger called for a driver, collected his own case with his

equipment, then hurried down to the canteen. He told Cope where he was going and what men he wanted to join him, and swallowed a cup of coffee. By the time he reached his car, both the driver and Fox were waiting; Fox with a large and a small vacuum cleaner and a box of envelopes, bottles and small jars. He got in the back with Roger, and within ten minutes they were at the shop. Being in the High Street, the police cars had aroused a lot of attention, and several policemen were on duty to make sure that the crowd did not encroach on to the roadway, and so hold up traffic. Their 'pass along, please, please pass along' seemed to have an edge to it. There must be a hundred people standing, staring and pushing. The Division had come to the front instead of the back—a bad tactical move, but probably there had been no way of avoiding it.

Roger went in, to find bald-headed Clayton, the manager of Anderson's, standing with a Divisional D.I., and looking as if he would soon go the way of old Anderson; two girls were standing just inside the shop, too, obviously shocked.

Roger remembered that the shop, with its crowded shelves and show cases, had always looked untidy; now it was in a state of chaos, because there was no controlling hand.

"Where is she?" he asked the Divisional man.

"On the second flight of stairs, sir," the man answered. "We thought it best not to move her."

"How was she found?"

"Mr. Clayton here—" the man began, but Clayton interrupted him with a wave of his hand, and spoke as if he were reciting blank verse.

"Every morning for twenty-five years Jennie's brought me a cup of tea as soon as I arrive. Every morning for twenty-five years. She unbolts the front door and I always unlock it and get ready by nine o'clock, then she comes down with my cup of tea. She didn't come down this morning, so I went to see if she was all right, and—and I found her lying there. I found her, dead." He closed his eyes and raised his hands, the tips of the thin fingers pressed together. "There is a curse upon this place," he declaimed. "There is the brand of Cain."

Roger said : "I can imagine how you feel, Mr. Clayton. Take it easy for a while. You're not opening the shop, I imagine?"

"No, sir, I am certainly not opening the shop."

"That's very wise," said Roger. "Look after him," he added to the Divisional man, and then went up the stairs, seeing two plain-clothes men on the first landing. He hurried past, turned, and saw the old woman's body. Except to make sure that she was dead, no one had touched it. From the landing ahead, a man was saying in a testy voice :

"Dammit, I haven't got all day to wait. She's dead and that's all about it."

"Sorry if I kept you, Doc," said Roger, cheerfully. "Just wanted to know if you could solve it for me."

"No need for your sarcasm, either." Old Dammit said, but his annoyance was only superficial. "Do you believe in coincidence?" he demanded.

Roger said : "Now what?"

"Remember that the pressure against the right side of the wind pipe was greater than that on the left in the Murray girl case?" asked old Dammit. "Well, this time the pressure's greater on the left. This woman was strangled from behind. Strangler probably left-handed. Not certain, mind you, but you ought to bear it in mind. Now I formally declare that life is extinct, and if you don't mind I'll go and see if I can do something for people who have a little time left in this wicked world."

11

SIMILARITIES

"Not much doubt that old Dammit's right," Fox remarked, as he and Roger straightened up from Jennie's body. "Wonder if there are any other similarities."

"If there are we'd better find 'em quick," Roger said. He glanced round at more Yard men who had arrived, some with measuring tapes and cameras. "You chaps get busy." He went upstairs to the big room, with the old woman's tiny bed in one corner, the chair facing the television and drawn up too closely, the whisky and the two glasses, hidden by the bottle. Roger bent down and sniffed the glasses, called Fox over, and said: "See if you can smell anything."

Fox sniffed in turn.

"Nowt," he announced. He stood back and stared at the shining glasses and the whisky bottle with its screw cap still tightly on, and said: "See what that means, Skipper?"

"You tell me."

"She knew who it was. She was expecting him, but he didn't get this far for his drink."

"Seems like it."

"She went down to open the door for him, and he killed her as she led the way upstairs," Fox continued. He rocked on his heels for a moment or two, and Roger went across to the television, breathed on and peered at the dialling knob, for prints. Then he went to the switch of the electric fire; his impression was these had been wiped off. "Skipper," Fox went on, "we could be wrong about that left-handed business."

"We could be wrong about most theories," Roger retorted dryly. "Why this one, in particular?" He had seen why almost as soon as he had looked closely at the body and the position on the stairs, but he was anxious to let Fox have his head; the sergeant looked like a good candidate for early promotion.

"At Alice Murray's flat, the man's right side was against the bed panel, and his left was free. He'd press harder with a free arm," Fox said. "The wall of the staircase here was against his right side—you can see that from the way the woman fell. The handrail's on the right side going up, the woman would be clutching that—I've seen her hauling herself upstairs. So the killer would have to get his main grip on the side away from the wall—the right. He would have room to move on the left, but be cramped on the other."

"Nice reasoning," Roger approved.

"Ta."

"As far as I could see downstairs there must have been some pretty clear footprints," Roger said, "and it looked as if the Divisional chaps covered them with some wood, we should be all right there. So get them and see if they match up with anyone we knew in the Murray case. I'll put Gill on to checking if there are any fingerprints which match up."

"And I'll get busy," Fox promised.

It was an hour before Roger left the flat and staircase, and he was pondering over the real or apparent similarities between this murder and the Murray girl's. Strangulation; uneven pressure of the hands; association with the same business and premises. He glanced in at the shop, to find Clayton standing and still talking in a drab, ceaseless monologue to the girls. Through the window Roger saw policemen moving the crowd on; some were attempting to get closer, to look inside. He went along to the cellar and the strongroom. Divisional men had been here, but they reported no signs of theft. Roger stood in the room, which was really a cellar, and saw the shelves piled with cheap jewellery and trinkets which hadn't been cleaned for years. There were five tall safes, all securely locked. The floor was dusty, and he could see footprints clearly as if they had been damp, and had carried away some dust, but he doubted if any could be identified. He saw some spots, each about the size of a sixpence, leading in a trail from the door towards one of the safes. This was taller and newer than most of the others. He went down on one knee, opened his case, and took out a small magnifying glass. He studied the spots carefully, then stood up and called to one of the men :

"Get these covered, will you? They look like rain spots to me, and it was raining last night. Those footprints could have been made with wet boots or shoes, too. Then fetch old Clayton."

Clayton came downstairs almost at once, and seemed eager to talk. In fact he talked so much that it was difficult to separate the real information from mournful words for words' sake.

"There were two sets of keys, Mr. West," he said. "One of them Mr. Anderson always had, and the other set was kept in the bank, just in case Mr. Anderson lost his, but it wasn't very likely, it really wasn't very likely at all. I was allowed to use the safe keys, but only Mr. Anderson or Mr. Julian had the strongroom door key, and they never let it out of their possession, I'm quite sure of that. Mr. Julian was in the process of sorting out the stock. I'm afraid that Mr. Anderson and I were rather over burdened with work and we had very little time for it, but Mr. Julian was a real *worker* . . . He used the new safe, the *Cannor*, that one over there."

Clayton pointed to the safe by the spots.

"And who had the keys after Mr. Anderson died?" Roger asked.

"Why, you know very well, I did," answered Clayton with dignity. "I would guard them with my life, Mr. West. As a matter of fact I have a special arrangement with the bank. I drop the keys into the night safe just along the road, and at a quarter to nine every morning I call at the back door of the bank and get them. There is always an official on duty at eight o'clock, to get ready for the morning rush and to count the night safe deposits."

"Did you collect the keys this morning?"

"Oh, yes, Mr. West. No one could possibly get in *here*."

Roger examined the handle of the safe closely, and began to feel uneasy, because the handle was unsmeared and probably free from prints. Surely the old man's should be there. Without betraying his suspicions, he asked:

"Will you open that safe, please?" and watched Clayton's unsteady fingers as he thrust in the large, complicated key, and turned the lock. The safe was at least forty years old so the word 'new' was a euphemism, but of its kind it was a good one, and there were no signs that anyone had attempted to force it.

The door was very heavy, and he helped Clayton to pull it. So, he was the first to see that the shelves were empty.

"But that's never been opened since Mr. Julian finished working on it," Clayton cried. "I've *never* opened it!"

*   *   *

It was a routine matter to arrange with the Governor of Brixton Prison to release Julian Anderson in police custody. Roger waited at the shop for him, and it was a little after twelve o'clock when he arrived. By now, the press were there in force, someone exclaimed: *"There's Julian Anderson!"* cameras flashed and there was a surge from the rear of the crowd. A reporter asked:

"Are they treating you all right in Brixton, Anderson?"

Julian didn't speak. Police forced a lane between the people, and he stepped inside the shop. Roger was waiting, met him civilly enough, and took him down to the strong-room. The girls watched from the side doorway of the shop itself, as if in awe. Old Clayton was still downstairs, and as Julian entered he came forward and put out his hands. Julian gripped them. Roger watched the man soon to stand trial for Alice Murray's murder very closely. Julian's face was thinner, and he looked older; his body was thinner, too, and he did not look so immaculate in the suit which had once made him like a tailor's dummy. He had acquired a kind of dignity, nevertheless. Roger had seen that before on people who were going through the rigours of awaiting trial for murder. 'Tragic figure' was still exactly the right description for him.

He let Clayton's hands go, and turned to Roger.

"I understand that there has been a robbery here, Mr. West."

"Yes," Roger said, and pointed to the open door. "Can you tell me how much of value there was in this particular safe?"

Julian replied, very softly: "It was crammed full, there was no spare room. It contained at least twenty thousand pounds worth of the best antique jewellery in our possession. I had sorted it out and put it aside for a visit from a Mr. Goldstein, from New York—he is an important buyer of this kind of jewellery, and makes a yearly visit to London. It was crammed full, Mr. West." Julian was beginning to feel the hurt, now. "It is a terrible loss, terrible."

"Was there a list of its contents?"

"There was one inside, and one in the office," Julian answered, and drew in a sharp breath. "Haven't you found the one in the office?"

"Mr. Julian, it was there yesterday, I swear it was," Clayton said. "I was looking for some old bills to see if I could make a reduction on a pair of earrings for a lady, and I actually saw it with my own eyes. But it isn't there now."

"Did you have a copy?" asked Roger.

Julian Anderson answered, as if this new blow had defeated him: "No, I didn't, God forgive me. I didn't. I thought that two were enough, Mr. West. There seemed no reason why I should take a third." He closed his eyes, and the lids were criss-crossed with little blue veins. "The goods were to be valued soon for insurance, at the moment there is only a single overall insurance cover, no special items were insured because none was of exceptional value."

Huskily, he went on: "What is happening here, Mr. West? Why should this place be robbed?"

"Possibly because the thieves knew that neither you nor your father had had time to make special arrangements, and it might have looked easy, with old Jennie here on her own," Roger replied, and paused. He always seemed to be turning the screw on this man, and never liked doing it. He studied the pale face closely, and it was obvious that Julian was beginning to realise there was another shock to come. "Jennie was murdered, Mr. Anderson. Strangled. And she was strangled by somebody whom she knew. Can you supply a full list of her acquaintances?"

Julian stood absolutely still.

"Oh, dear God, dear God," breathed Clayton.

There was nothing to read from Anderson's expression except shock and grief. He pressed his pale hands to his forehead, and swallowed hard, then he answered in a voice that was barely audible:

"I think I can, Mr. West. I think I can." A glint sparked into his eyes, and there was a firmer tone in his voice: "Mr. West—couldn't this have been done by the same person?" He didn't add: 'And if it was, then you know I didn't kill Alice.'

"Why should the same person murder both Jennie and Miss Murray?" demanded Roger.

Julian said, in that more eager voice:

"I've had a lot of time to think, Mr. West, and I realise that I haven't long to save myself. I have been trying to imagine why anyone could conceivably want to kill Alice, and there is one possible motive. It wasn't any use talking about it before because it looked like a wild guess, as nothing had been stolen. But now this has happened—" He broke off, raised his hands and clenched them, and there was a touch of colour on his pale cheeks. "Alice had access to all the keys! My father and I trusted her implicitly. Now if some man made up to her only to get hold of those keys, wouldn't he want her dead once he got them?"

He broke off, as if hope dazzled him.

"If there was such a man, we'll find him," Roger said.

* * *

He wished that he were on his own, driving back to the Yard, instead of with a driver and Fox, who was sitting beside him. Fox had discovered little more, and was anxious to examine everything he had found more closely. Roger checked that nothing new had come in at his office, had a word with Cope, who seemed contented enough, went downstairs to the canteen for some sausages and mash and a steamed raisin pudding, then went back to see Fox. Fox had a dry-looking sandwich and an empty coffee cup on his bench; he would work night and day if necessary.

"What's new?" inquired Roger.

"Not a bloody thing," answered Fox. "I've checked with *Fingerprints*, and the only dabs in that room were the old woman's. Nothing on the glasses, the television or the door handle. No stranger's prints anywhere, for that matter; our chap wore gloves. Can't get a thing from the footprints, except a guess at the size of the man's foot: he takes nines or tens."

"Fairly large?"

"Large," rejoined Fox. "Those spots you saw were probably rain spots. I've scraped some up and analysed the scrapings as far as I can—there doesn't seem to be more than a speck or two of dirt from the cellar floor, and a tiny bit of metal—nothing that seemed to have been carried in on the man's shoes. This joker's no fool. If you ask me, our main hope is to find someone who saw him. Had anything in from the boys doing the knock-and-natter job?"

"Can't expect anything until this evening unless we get a lot of luck," Roger said. "Found anything at all to link this up with the Murray girl?"

"Only the pressure on the neck, the sex and the Anderson tie-in," answered Fox.

Roger moved across to a section on a shelf marked: *Alice*

Murray. In boxes on the shelf were different exhibits which Fox had obtained—including the matches with prints, the quarter-pound chocolate boxes with the prints carefully preserved and a small plastic envelope with a label twice its size, marked: *Steel Filings found on carpet in A.M.'s room.* There was little doubt that someone had been in the room some time after working with a lathe, turning steel, that some of the filings had fallen on to his boots or shoes, lodged in the welts, and shaken off when he had moved about the room. Fox had made sure that these were analysed, and Roger read: *Case-hardened mild steel, 18% chromium, 8% nickel, tensile strength about 40 tons per square inch.*

"Charley," Roger said, sharply.

"What's that, Skipper?" Charley Fox was sorting through dust taken from the staircase at the Anderson place, and from old Jennie's room.

"Know what is made of steel like this?"

"Like what?" Fox turned his head; in profile, he was positively simian. "Oh, those. No, I can't say—"

He broke off.

"Keys," Roger said.

"*Gawd!*" breathed Fox.

"Keys," Roger repeated. "And keys were used last night, although the only two sets known to be in existence were at that bank, one in its vaults and one in the night safe. So there's a third set in existence. The set must have been made from impressions of the originals or from the originals themselves. Julian's quite right, too—Alice Murray had access to them. How are the odds on coincidence?"

"Getting longer," Fox declared. "If only I could get one piece of iron filing at the shop, anything that would really tie the two jobs up." He frowned, turned round to face Roger squarely, and said: "I don't know that I like this job much, Mr. West."

"I can't say I do," Roger concurred. "The circumstantial case against Julian Anderson is as strong as ever, but we could still have the wrong man."

"Think the Public Prosecutor's office would withdraw the charge if we told 'em it was weaker than we thought?"

Roger said, slowly, thoughtfully: "It would be a hell of a job to persuade them to unless we could give very good reasons. The case is being built up on evidence we supplied, sound evidence, too. We haven't found a thing to disprove any of it. It stands up just as well today as it did a month ago—and it will stand up just as well at the Old Bailey, if it gets that far. See what we'd be up against?"

"Red tape!" Fox replied, disgustedly.

"Not just red tape," Roger reasoned. "We've built up a case, and it's a good one, because we thought we had the right man. Now we're seeing it from the defendant's angle of bias. All we've got to break it down is an uneasy feeling that we might be wrong. If we could get a tiny iron or steel filing to prove that the man who killed old Jennie killed that girl, it would be different." He rubbed his chin, very slowly, and went on: "We could be wrong in sympathising with Julian Anderson, too. He could be working with someone else. He could have arranged for these keys to be cut. The fact that he was caught for the Murray girl's murder doesn't mean that he didn't have an accomplice who is carrying on with the job."

"The job being what?" Fox demanded.

"Remember that when the Murray girl was killed, no one realised that old Anderson would die of a heart attack," Roger pointed out. "This is a junk shop in some ways, there's one overall insurance cover for thirty thousand pounds and little to prove the actual value of any goods stolen. Julian might be in the racket. It's even possible that Julian and his father were planning to rob their own shop, or else that Julian planned to rob his own father. Alice might have discovered that, so his future would be at stake in case she talked. Julian would be pretty sick if he'd been forced to kill the girl he loved, and then discovered that the shock of the conspiracy killed the old man. He'd be the tragic figure all right."

After a pause, Fox said: "I don't know whether I feel any better or not." He came over, and picked up the empty chocolate box which had a piece of transparent plastic fastened over the print, to preserve it; there was no real need for the photographs were in the files, but Fox always liked to keep the original evidence as long as possible. "If we could find the mate to that print we might get places. I've checked with *Records* until they hate the sight of me. Come across it one of these days, I daresay," he added, and scowled. "I wonder if Julian *is* foxing us. You want to know something?" he added, and there was a gleam in his eyes. "I was one of the don't-do-away-with-hanging boys, this is the first time I'm glad a chap convicted for murder isn't always hanged. If Julian A. gets sent down for life, he could always get a Queen's Pardon."

"It's a thought," Roger said, and realised how heavily doubt weighed on the other man's mind. He went back to the exhibits Fox was preparing on the Jennie murder, picked up the dust from the rain spot scrapings, and said:

"Sent any of this up to the lab for analysis?"

"Yes."

Roger peered at it, and after a long pause, went on:

"Send this up, too, Charley. Make sure we don't slip up over a trifle."

"Suits me," Fox agreed.

Roger looked in at Anderson's shop on the way home that evening. No other news had come in, not a single witness appeared to have seen anyone approach the front or the back of the shop the previous night; it had been too wet and windy for people to look about them much. Old Clayton wanted to close the shop for the next day or two, but said that his conscience worried him—if they stopped trading it might mean that the eventual buyer would pay less for the goodwill. No list was found of the stolen goods. Julian Anderson was helping to prepare a list of Jennie's acquaintances, and Clayton was to check and add to it, but there was nothing very promising in that line of inquiry yet. Julian was also drawing up a list of the set pieces of jewellery which he could remember were in the safe; this was likely to be only a rough guide, but could be sent round to jewellers and dealers, as well as to police stations up and down the country; a single set piece found on the market might help them.

One trouble was, of course, that a lot of this kind of jewellery was sold abroad.

At home, before getting out of his car, he made a note: *Check if any American buyers of antique jewellery are in London*; the years were teaching him that it was not wise to rely on memory. It was about half past six when he got in, quite an early evening. There was no sign of the boys, but the radio was on, and Janet was upstairs, singing to keep it company. He called out and hurried up, and she met him at the door of the bedroom. One glance was enough to tell him that she was excited.

"Darling, I've been over the Montifiore's house!" she greeted. "They are asking *seven* thousand five hundred, but Mrs. Monty said that she thinks her husband would come down a lot. It's a *wonderful* place. We'd have to go all over London to find one better."

"My sweet," said Roger, "at seven thousand pounds or so, we'd have to! It's no use loading ourselves up with expenses we can't meet. Six thousand's the absolute limit."

"Oh, I know," said Janet, quite casually. "It's impossible at the price, but—well, if it doesn't sell in the next few weeks, he's bound to lower his price. Every time I pass the place I shall have my heart in my mouth, in case the *For Sale* board is down."

12

OFFER

JOHN PAYNE kept his ear very close to the ground during the next few days, to find out whether a list of the Anderson goods had been circulated. None had. There had been a few inquiries from the police and several pieces had been mentioned, but no more than one piece out of twenty or thirty. By listening intently and not missing a thing when he was with others in the trade, he found out what these named pieces were; and it was a simple matter to take them out of their settings and sell them; the gold and silver of the settings could be melted down and sold at a good price. He was careful not to offer too much of anything for the next three weeks. By that time, he felt sure that the police had absolutely nothing to go on over the old woman's murder. No arrest had been made, and it was two weeks since the case had been mentioned in the newspapers.

Payne had almost forgotten that he had killed Jennie, and Alice only came into his thoughts occasionally, when something quite unusual reminded him of her. At home, the high spirits which had followed his 'best deal of my life' had never really faded. Gwen was busy house-hunting. Maurice was inclined to be careless with his ten shillings a week pocket money, obviously reasoning that he would probably get more in an emergency. Hilda bought two new hats, and—coincidentally no doubt—acquired a new boy friend, and spent three evenings in one week out with him; Hilda would meet a regular boy friend before long. Payne left it to Gwen to worry about what their daughter did when she was out so late in the evenings, and Gwen seemed to be quite sure that Hilda could look after herself.

It was three and a half weeks after the shop murder, on

a Saturday, when Gwen came in from the morning's shopping heavily-laden, rather late, and with a purposefulness
which told Payne that she had a lot on her mind. He had
been in the workshop, taking some of the settings off Anderson jewellery. He was going to offer a quantity of it to old
Benoni next Monday, and wanted to take along as much as
possible. It was fascinating work, altering some settings so
that they could not easily be identified, and he had always
been a good craftsman. Only Gwen ever came to the workshop without knocking, and it didn't surprise him when he
saw her framed in the doorway. It was a cold, bright day
early in March.

"Hallo, ducks," Payne said. "I've got a piece of jade here
that will just match the colour of your eyes. Like to have it?"

"In future, I want mink and diamonds," Gwen retorted,
and came in, let the door swing to on its hydraulic hinge,
looked at the jade which glowed balefully under the bright
electric light, and said with more interest : "It is nice, and
Hilda would love it. Jack, I think I've found it!"

"Found what?"

"The house."

"Go away with you," Payne jeered. "You've been finding
that every day for the past month!"

"I mean it, this time."

"Nothing over twenty thousand pounds!"

"This one is seven and a half."

"I should think we could go that high," conceded Payne,
and turned to face her, realising how earnest she was. Excitement and eagerness gave her an added vitality. "Where
is it?"

"In Chelsea, of course."

He thought: *Pity*. But the district did not worry him as
it had a few weeks ago. "On the river?"

"Just about a perfect position." He had never known
Gwen so enthusiastic about anything. "It's on the corner
of Bell Street and Greenways Avenue—not far from Manville Street."

"*Where?*" Payne demanded, and the street name stabbed through him, bringing fear, bringing the urgent desire to say: 'It's impossible!' He had made Gwen see that it had really shaken him, and now had to find a reason. He gulped, grinned, and said: "Not in that slum!"

"Don't be ridiculous," Gwen retorted sharply. "It's not a slum. It's one of the best residential parts of Chelsea, and there aren't many places with fairly modern houses in them. This one is exactly right. It was built in nineteen thirty-seven, when building materials were really good, and . . ."

She talked not only persuasively, but with the kind of purposefulness which told Payne that he would have a difficult task to turn her off this house. Was it worth worrying about? At first, there had been the fear of danger, the possibility that he would be recognised, but the heat was well off by now. He had no sentimental regard for Alice Murray, and now knew that he would think less and less often about her as time went on. He knew Bell Street extremely well, and there was no need to pass Number 24 Manville Street to get to the buses or to get to the river.

". . . and I've arranged to meet the agent there this afternoon, at half past three," Gwen announced. "Maurice will be watching Fulham play, but Hilda's coming—she's had a tiff with her boy friend. And," Gwen added, putting her head on one side and staring at him intently, "you had better like it, lover-boy."

"I still think it's a poor district," Payne said; it would be folly to give in too easily.

"Don't talk out of the back of your neck," retorted Gwen. "It's only five minutes from the new technical school, too, exactly right for Maurice. Lunch will be half an hour late," she added, "but I'll have it dished up by half past one sharp."

She went off, briskly.

Payne said, sotto voce: "Well, if she wants it she'd better have it." The way she had looked when she had come in, and the gleam in her eyes, remained with him. He had been so busy planning and thinking about the main job that he had not given Gwen much thought in the past few weeks. It was time he did. He was doing all this for her, wasn't he? He stood with the piece of jade in his right hand, the gold setting in the other, and stared into the stone. Was he doing it for Gwen? He had told himself all along that he was : she *needed* beautiful clothes and furs and jewellery, she was a woman in a million. He found his thoughts slipping back to the time when he had first met her, and had promised her the earth. Even then, she had half-mocked him.

"You make sure we don't starve, Jack, and that's all you need to worry about."

Well, they hadn't starved. In fact, he had done fairly well, but all the time he had felt that sense of insecurity and of failure, because he had not given Gwen what he had promised. Deep down, there was always the feeling, perhaps the fear, that in spite of her banter she had been disappointed. She had never reproached him, but it had been Gwen who had first called the house a rabbit-hutch; Gwen who had gone up to the January sales and fought to get the good clothes for the children, for herself and for him; Gwen who had always kept the family a cut above the ordinary. So it was true to say that he had really done all this for her; she had kept urging him on.

He wondered what she would think if she knew what he had done.

He had an eerie, shivery feeling that there would be a very different light in her eyes, that she would be horrified.

What would Hilda think?

What would Maurice think?

Payne found his mouth going dry, felt the cold striking along his back to his head, his legs and his arms, although it wasn't cold in here. He had never posed that question before, and now it seemed to scream at him. What *would* they think? Would they shrink away from him? Could anything make Gwen do that? He looked down at his hands, so strong, clean and lean, used to handling the tools of his trade, each finger very powerful. There was as much strength in the left as in the right one, too. He pictured them, curling round, crooking themselves, burying themselves into human flesh. He remembered the way his fingers had seemed to embed themselves into Alice's fair neck, when for a moment he had not been able to free them; and he remembered how dry and sinewy the old woman's neck had been.

He was sweating all over.

He thought: *They mustn't ever know. They needn't ever know.*

And—only the best was good enough for Gwen. He had always known that, and deep down inside him there had been that determination to get it for her. There had been no other way, and—what good had money been to old Anderson? Didn't Julian have enough? They wouldn't hang Julian—after a few years in prison they would release him, as they always did, these days; society had gone soft.

They would hang him, John Payne, if they ever proved that he had killed these two women, because two murders still meant the gallows.

What was the matter with him? Why was he thinking like this? Why had Gwen sparked off such a morbid train of thought? He stood quite still except for a little spasm of shivering which seemed to start from his feet and work upwards, and told himself that he must get on top of himself; he had a little time to spare, yet. He made himself put the jade and the setting down on the bench, took out a handkerchief and wiped his forehead and face, but his whole body seemed clammy; what he wanted was a bath. Well, why not? He had been working very hard, and there had been too much strain at his nerves. He could relax for half an hour, have a good meal, go and see this house and see whether Gwen was as serious as she seemed to be; then they would go up to the West End somewhere for tea. Maurice could meet them afterwards, and they could go to a show. It would be a real family evening out, now that Hilda had broken it off with the boy friend, and there was no reason why it shouldn't be one of the happiest they had had for years. It was some time since he had blown ten quid in the West End.

This is what he would do; he felt better already!

He went out, locked the workshop door carefully behind him, slid the key into his pocket, and began to whistle. He hoped that he looked all right, now. Gwen wasn't in the kitchen and that was a good thing; there was little risk of being seen. He went whistling up the stairs, feeling better and bolder every second, and turned into the bathroom. There she was, glancing round from the handbasin to look at him, water running over her hands.

"Hi, ducks," he said. "Time for me to have a bath before lunch?"

"Just about," answered Gwen, and looked at him curiously. She always seemed to be able to see through his thoughts, it was almost impossible to deceive her. "How are you feeling, Jack?"

"Never better!"

"Listen, lover-boy, you don't have to put on an act with me," Gwen said. "You've been working all the hours that God gave you lately. I don't want to buy a new house if it means you're going to have to work yourself to the bone in order to pay for it."

"No, it isn't that," he assured her eagerly, and he could have laughed, she was so wide of the mark. She knew there was plenty on his mind, but would never dream what it was. "It's just that I've been working up to a climax for years! These jewels are *exactly* what we want. That American buyer will be in London next week, and a lot depends on the actual figure he'll pay me for the stock from that Watford place, but whatever it is, it won't interfere with our plans. We can afford that house, and we can afford—"

"Let's get the house and get it properly furnished, and then see what comes next," Gwen said practically. "You're sure, Jack? You haven't got into debt, have you?"

"Good God, no!"

His vehemence made Gwen laugh.

"That question even surprised you, so I'll believe you," she said. "Don't be more than twenty minutes." She dodged past him, rightly guessing that he would try to grab her, and went laughing down the stairs. So she had been aware that something was the matter, she had been watching him closely. It was always essential to have a good convincing story for her; there were no flies on Gwen!

He began to run the bath.

A little before three o'clock, he turned the car into Bell Street, his mind shadowed by the fact that when he had last come along here, it had been on Maurice's bicycle. He drew up towards the end of the street, in the parking space which he had used for the bicycle; it must be about the same spot. He pulled up, feeling a little queasy, but Gwen was already opening the door, and Hilda was squeezing out of the back door of the small car, sharing her mother's excitement.

Gwen looked down at the kerb, and called:

"You're a bit out at the back, Jack."

He waved acknowledgment, and took the car forward. That gave him a few seconds to recover, and also gave him something to do. When he reversed, Gwen called: "*Too far!*" and a moment later he bumped the kerb. He went forward again, then reversed perfectly, and as he got out, Gwen was grumbling:

"You'll have to take your test again if you go on at this rate, and as for buying a Jaguar—"

"Rolls-Royce!"

"*I'll* settle for a Bentley," Hilda put in. "Dad, *do* come on." She and her mother went ahead, arm-in-arm, towards the house on the corner.

This stood in its own grounds, with smooth lawns on the Bell Street side. There was a brick built garage, and a carriage-way with two entrances. The house itself was of two storeys, built of red brick, and with wooden beams showing, an imitation Tudor style which was not displeasing. It looked solid, and probably seemed larger than it was because it was so much larger than most of its neighbours. Farther along the street towards King's Road dozens of houses stood in their own small plot of land, each with neat hedge, most with small trees in the front gardens. Some almond and cherry blossom trees were already out, beautiful pink umbrellas. There were five in the garden of Cornerways, and they softened the brick and lent both quality and attractiveness which might otherwise have been missing. The carriage-way was made of crazy paving, and Payne saw that this was well-laid; the place had a pre-war solidity which it was hard to come by these days.

He liked what he first saw of it.

He did not like grey-haired eagle-nosed Mrs. Montysomething who showed them over the house. He did not like the furniture, which was all dark mahogany, heavy and Victorian, and reminded him of old Anderson's flat. But he liked the rooms, and could see that very little new decoration would have to be done for a year or two; give Gwen a newly decorated bedroom and sitting-room, and she would be crowing over all the neighbours. He saw her peering into cupboards and corners as if already deciding where to put the pots and pans, the linen and the cleaning equipment. The kitchen, which might so easily have been old fashioned, was in fact modern, bright and gay.

The one snag, if snag it was, was in Mrs. Monty-something. She seemed determined to run the house down, and certainly wasn't trying to sell it. Gwen seemed to ignore this, but the little woman annoyed Payne; he wanted to shut her mouth.

After half an hour, they had finished.

"You won't keep us long making up your mind, will you?" asked Mrs. Montifiore. "We've had several offers already, and my husband and I are most anxious to get everything settled quickly. We have a cottage in Devon all ready for us, and we want to move there as soon as we can."

"What's your lowest price?" asked Payne, brusquely.

"The price we are asking is—"

"I know, you're asking seven and a half thousand," Payne interrupted, and he noticed the way that Gwen stared, trying to stop him from speaking with such abruptness; but the old fool annoyed him. In a way, she reminded him of Jennie. "I want to know your lowest price."

Mrs. Montifiore said, tartly : "Seven thousand two hundred and fifty pounds."

Payne said : "I'll buy it."

Gwen gasped. Hilda's eyes looked as if a silver light shone from them, and clasped her hands together ecstatically. Even the little old grey parrot of a woman seemed shaken, and she asked as if doubtfully :

"You mean, you are offering seven thousand two hundred and fifty pounds now ?"

"Yes," said Payne, and took out his cheque book. "Here's a cheque for the two hundred and fifty to settle the deal, and I'll instruct my solicitors to get busy at once. That's if it's all right with you."

"Why, yes—y-yes, of course," stammered Mrs. Montifiore, and for the first time she looked really pleased. She gave a little laugh, and added : "I'll be glad to give you a receipt, Mr. Payne. When—when would you want completion ?"

"Quick as possible," Payne replied. "The quicker the better from our point of view, we would like to move in during the spring, too. A lot wants doing to the place, so we'll need a month or so to work in. It's a deal, then ?"

"Yes, of course," declared Mrs. Montifiore. "Forgive me if I seemed a little confused, but I am not used to people who make up their minds so quickly."

"In my business, you have to," Payne said. He took out a ball pen and wrote the cheque, as Mrs. Montifiore said :

"Would you like to have a look round by yourselves, while I make a cup of tea ? My husband will be back before long. He's gone to see a football match, but he promised to be home by five or five fifteen, and it's getting on for five o'clock now." She behaved as if she were really fussed, and when Payne handed her the cheque, she swallowed hard, and went rather dazedly towards the kitchen.

"You fool, if you'd stood out a bit you could have got it for five hundred less," Gwen hissed, but there was no real reproach in her voice.

Payne looked her up and down, telling himself that he had never seen her looking more beautiful. For that matter, Hilda took a lot of beating, too. He winked, made a thumbs up sign, and said:

"I always promised you a big house and mink, honey, and Johnnie Payne always keeps his promises. Okay?"

Gwen put her arms round him, Hilda put hers round them both, there was a funny little moment of excitement and confusion, in which Payne felt quite choky. He was sure that he had done the right thing; he would never regret giving Gwen what she wanted, and there was another thing to consider, too; living in a house like this would put Hilda's marriage chances up, this was a higher income neighbourhood than where they were living now.

It was working out perfectly.

They looked down into the street from a front bedroom; several boys, on bicycles, were fooling about on the other side of the road. When they went downstairs and looked out of the front room there, the boys were still in sight but half hidden by the privet hedge. Gwen was studying the curtains, knowing that she could buy them at valuation, tugging them and making sure that they were in reasonable condition; there were certainly no flies on Gwen!

Payne noticed that at every chance she got, Hilda looked out of the window towards the boys. They were a bit young for her, surely. He was in an expansive mood, however, and if he could give the kid five minutes pleasure, why not? And the boys weren't too young to appreciate the finer points of Hilda as an eyeful.

He suggested that they should look in the garden.

"You and Hilda can," Gwen said. "I want to see every-thing there is to see here while I've got the chance."

Payne opened the front door, and at once realised that the boys were deliberately fooling around on their machines in order to give the callers at Cornerways the onceover. There were three, all in their late teens; one of them might be nearly twenty. He was very broad, had a clean cut look, and turned the front wheel of the cycle about as if he were the chief performer of a circus act.

He kept glancing this way.

Suddenly he stopped pretending that he wasn't interested, and stared openly at Hilda. Hilda stared as openly back. Payne glanced at her, saw that she was beginning to smile, and found himself grinning. That was the way Gwen had caught him, with that come-hither look which had made her seem the most desirable creature in the world. Hilda had dressed for this occasion, so she was looking at her best. The way the gaze of the boy and girl met and challenged each other was quite remarkable. The boy gave a most attractive grin, and waved.

Hilda waved back.

"Think you're going to like living here?" asked Payne.

"I'm going to love it!" Hilda cried.

Mrs. Montifiore called out that tea was ready. Almost at the same moment a small car pulled in at one of the entrance gates, and Mr. Montifiore got out of the car. His wife greeted him, calling out in a carrying voice:

"Hurry up, George! Mr. Payne is going to buy the house."

*   *   *

"Hey, Scoop!" exclaimed Richard West, "did you hear that? Those people are going to buy the place. What a swizz! Mum will be really fed up when she hears about this."

Scoopy didn't answer.

"Scoop, why don't you say something?" demanded Richard.

"What about?" asked Scoopy. He was staring across at the house, seeing the front door close on the man and the girl; the girl went in last, and just before closing it, deliberately turned and looked round; there was no doubt that she meant it for him. He continued to look at the house, but switched his gaze towards the front room; a moment later the girl appeared at a window. The older woman was with her, and they pretended to be admiring the lawn and the almond blossom, but in fact the girl was eyeing Scoopy again.

"Oh, stop trying to be a wolf!" Richard exclaimed, in disgust. "They're going to buy the house, the clots. Mum is just about going to hit the roof when she hears."

"Going to buy—you mean they're going to *live* here?" asked Scoopy, and seemed to wake to life. But he had none of the concern of his brother, none for his mother; he looked absolutely delighted. "Are you sure? I didn't hear what they said."

"You would have if you hadn't been making eyes at that dame," said a boy from a neighbouring house. He was grinning. "I must say she had something."

"She had *every*thing," declared Scoopy.

"If you ask me, she hasn't got many manners at all," said Richard, with a great show of virtue. "The way she ogled you was absolutely disgusting."

"Don't talk out of the back of your neck, Fish," Scoopy retorted.

"Well, it was."

" 'Ogled' is a jolly good word," the other boy conceded, in mock admiration. "I agreed with Scoop, though, that doll has just about everything. How old would you think she was, Scoop?"

"Oh, about seventeen, I suppose."

"I would say she's at least twenty-one—quite old," said Richard, cuttingly.

"You'll be making out she's a grandmother next," said Scoopy, and won a sudden grin from his brother, who was seldom in a bad mood for long. Then a woman called out from along the street :

"Eric ! I want you to go to the shops for me."

"Here we go again," said the other boy, and promptly cycled off, calling resignedly : "Coming, Mum." His mother disappeared, while Scoopy and Richard sat on their bicycles, Scoopy still trying to catch a glimpse of the blonde. Although they could just see people moving about in the sitting-room of Cornerways, none of them was near enough the window to be seen clearly.

"Come on, Scoop," Richard urged. "You can't be here when they come out again, the girl will think that you can't think of anything else but sex."

Scoopy chuckled, a moment later Richard grinned, and they turned their bicycles towards home. Although it was Saturday, their father was not back from the Yard, but they were used to him being at work on Saturdays and Sundays. Only now and again could they be sure of a full week-end together. They heard their mother playing the piano in the sitting-room; it was the best piece of furniture they had, a wedding present from a close friend who had gone to live in the United States.

They wheeled the bicycles round to the back, tip-toed through the house until they were back in the front garden; and looked through the window, listening and watching. Janet West played light and lively pieces from her own childhood. *In a Monastery Garden*, *Tip-Toe Through the Tulips*, *Tea for Two*; then she paused, hesitated, and poised her hands above the piano, unconscious of how attractive she was. Suddenly her hands plunged downwards, and she began to play rock-and-roll, but she kept missing notes, laughing, missing more, and finally began a nonsense medley. The boys couldn't keep their laughter back. She started, swivelled round on the stool and shook her fist at them. In a few minutes they were all together in the front rom, singing while Janet played. *Old Man River*, *The Stein Song*, *Coal Black Mammy*, and others which the boys had learnt from Janet. They were swinging along into *Felix Keeps on Walking* when Roger's deep voice sounded in the doorway, joining in a kind of basso profundo. There was only a moment's pause before they went on with the song until, pretending exhaustion, Janet stopped playing.

"We'll have complaints from the neighbours next," she said. "How far along the road could you hear that, Roger?"

"Oh, only just round the corner," Roger said, airily. "Talking of neighbours, Mrs. Montifiore has just been saying goodbye to a family so fervently that I wouldn't be surprised if she hasn't sold the house."

Janet's face fell; "Oh, *no*!"

After a pause, Richard said, with a brave attempt to sound as if it didn't matter :

"She has, Mum, as a matter of fact. Scoop and I heard her saying so. We happened to be passing the house just as she was talking to the man. Didn't we, Scoop?"

"Er—yes."

"Oh, *hell*!" exclaimed Janet, and all the merriment and the happiness was washed away; obviously she was really upset. "I'd set such store by having Cornerways. Only this morning Mrs. Montifiore said that she was sure that her husband would come down to six thousand five hundred and—" She broke off.

"And you said you were sure you could needle your husband up to six thousand five," said Roger, dryly.

"Well, five hundred pounds spread over fifteen years—" Janet began, then dropped her hands by her sides, and went on glumly : "Well, if it's sold, it's sold."

"We'll probably find one just as good," Roger said.

"Oh, you never really wanted Cornerways," Janet said in vexation, and Roger smothered a grin. "You pretended to be interested because you knew how keen I was, but I knew you would never really agree to buying it. And we've lived in this—in this *hutch* for over twenty-one years."

The boys were heading for the door.

"Well, we ought to get washed for supper," Richard said, virtuously.

"Want anything from the shops, Mum?" inquired Scoopy.

"No, I don't, and you know perfectly well that I don't," Janet snapped; then quite suddenly she realised that Roger was trying not to grin at her, and that the boys were anxious to leave because, if they stayed, they would start laughing. "Fools!" she exclaimed. "It's true, all the same. You were never keen on it."

"I'd be happier if we stopped at six thousand," Roger admitted, "and you would be, too, really."

"You never know," interpolated Richard, "these people might get fed up with the place, and sell again next year. Mum was saying that the winter is really the best time to buy, prices are always lower then, and we might actually get the house for six thousand."

"That's enough of your blarney," Janet said.

"I say," Scoopy put in, his eyes glowing, "there was an absolutely smashing girl with the people who've bought Cornerways. Wasn't she, Fish? Absolutely smashing. I haven't seen a more beautiful girl in my life."

Janet gasped.

Roger said. "You will."

"Scoop, you're far too young—" Janet began, urgently.

"Dammit, I can *think* about a girl, can't I?" Scoopy demanded, warmly.

After a moment, Janet said in a much milder voice:

"Yes, Scoop, of course you can. The one thing I ask is that if you see a girl you like you'll tell us—just as you've told us about this one. That's all that really matters."

"What did you think of this paragon?" asked Roger of Richard, into a pause.

"Well, as a matter of fact, I thought she was a bit flamboyant," Richard answered, earnestly. "She—er—she was a bit what you call Sabrina-ish, if you know what I mean."

"I know exactly what you mean," Roger said. "Off with

the pair of you!" He grinned as they went out, but Janet was frowning. He went across to her and slid an arm round her waist. "Forget it," he counselled. "It's the growing-up process, and it's no use trying to stop it or worrying about it."

Janet didn't answer.

"Come on, sweet," Roger urged.

"Oh, I'm not worried," Janet said, quickly. "Not really worried, anyhow. I knew we would have to face up to this sooner or later, but it's come so unexpectedly. When they went out at lunchtime, I thought they were two schoolboys with no thought for anything but games, sports and the pictures. Now—well, it's a bit of a shock, darling."

"Bad day for shocks," Roger said. "What with the news about the house, too. I suppose the boys are right."

"They usually are," said Janet, and after a pause, went on : "I wonder who's bought Cornerways."

13

GOOD PRICE

Benoni looked at the collection of Regency jewellery, as well as several exquisite old French sets, through the black watchmaker's glass which he invariably screwed into his left eye when examining jewels. He was a long time, sitting at a small bench in a room behind his shop, and turning each piece this way and that, as if he were making quite sure that there was not the slightest blemish. He was deliberately trying to agitate Payne, of course, but Payne knew his tactics well. The longer he looked, the more he pulled down his lips, the less he would offer, and the more likely the seller would be to accept a low price. It was his kind of bargaining.

This Monday morning, however, Payne wasn't in a mood to stand a lot of it; he wanted a quick sale, and cash in his pocket. Old Benoni always paid in cash, and that set Payne thinking.

Where did he keep it? He couldn't do a big trade every day, and yet he never failed to have enough for any particular deal available. Payne found himself looking about the little room, because he could not bear to stand and watch Benoni examine jewellery which *could* be identified as that taken from the Anderson strongroom. There was practically no likelihood of that, of course, but it could happen. It seemed to him that Benoni was taking much longer than usual, too. It was conceivable that he knew more about Anderson's stock than anyone else in London.

Why didn't the old fool make up his mind?

Benoni sniffed, pulled a face, and then put the last of the pieces down on his bench. He took the glass out of his eye, rubbed the eye which began to water a little, and then moistened his lips.

"How much do you want for this, Mr. Payne?" he inquired.

Payne thought: He's going to take it all right, he'll take it. There were about ten thousand pounds worth of jewels on the bench in front of him, and Benoni had once talked of being able to give a better-than-average price through the American, Goldstein. He never made the first offer, so there was nothing at all unusual in his inquiry, but the first offer was important. Payne had to put a reasonable price on this, and not appear to be too eager.

At last, he said: "Seven thousand."

Benoni didn't answer.

"It's fair enough," Payne urged, then warned himself not to be too eager to sell. "I'd get more if I went to the Yank myself."

"Yes, undoubtedly," Benoni said. "But Mr. Goldstein only deals with individuals he knows well, he has to be sure that they are absolutely trustworthy."

Payne barked: "What do you mean by that?"

"Isn't it obvious?" Benoni asked mildly. "Mr. Goldstein cannot buy from casual acquaintances, he has to take all of his purchases through Customs, and they are liable to be examined on both sides of the Atlantic. Seven thousand pounds is far too much." He shook his head slowly, and looked up at Payne beneath his shaggy grey eyebrows. It was impossible to predict what he was going to offer, but he was a reasonable man who didn't play around too much. There seemed to be something odd about him today, but perhaps that was because this was a bigger deal than he usually handled with Payne.

"Come on, let's hear from you," Payne urged.

Benoni said, very, very softly: "I will pay you three thousand pounds in cash for it, Mr. Payne."

Payne exclaimed: "Don't be a bloody fool!"

The old man did not change his expression, and kept looking at him through his pince-nez. Payne had not realised how clear and pale a blue his eyes were; in fact he could hardly see Benoni's face, those eyes seemed to have a strange, compelling quality, as if he were trying to will Payne to accept the offer.

"Three thousand pounds," he repeated.

"But they're worth nine thousand at least! Even at my figure you're getting them cheap."

"Am I?" asked Benoni, and after a long pause, he went on: "What about the risk?"

Payne raised his hands, the palms outwards, as if to fend off an attack. He had been half prepared, and yet the shock was very great. He had to fight it away, had to behave as if he didn't know what the old man was talking about. Just a second or two too late, he said:

"Risk? What the devil are you talking about?"

"Mr. Payne," said Benoni, without a change of tone, "I will give you three thousand pounds for these jewels, not one penny more. I will pay you another three thousand, cash, if you can supply me with an equivalent quantity of the same value. I shall not be able to sell them all at once, you know that as well as I do."

"It's barefaced robbery!" Payne said. He found himself trembling and on the point of shouting, but a little hope was dawning in his mind. Six thousand pounds was a lot of money, quite enough to put plenty down on the house that Gwen had set her heart on, and to buy what new furniture they needed; and he had some cash by him, the usual profit on turnover. Moreover, he would still have some of the jewels from Anderson's shop, sets which he would release over a long period. He realised that he had made a tactical mistake in offering too much to old Benoni at one time, but he didn't give that much thought. After all, the important thing was to find a quick market.

On the other hand, there were others who dealt with this Goldstein.

"You can walk out of here with the money," Benoni told him, temptingly.

Payne barked: "No. I'll take six thousand for this lot,

not a penny less. It's worth more, and I can get more if I sell it in smaller quantities." When Benoni did not respond, he went on : "You know that as well as I do."

"Yes," Benoni said. "You are quite right, Mr. Payne, you can get more for it if you sell it in smaller quantities and if you are prepared to take the risk."

"There isn't any risk! It's stuff I bought from an old cove out at Watford, he wanted a quick turnover."

"I see," said Benoni, and shrugged. "Well, then, I am sorry that we cannot do business, Mr. Payne."

"You're throwing money away."

"Possibly."

"Look here, let's settle for five thousand," Payne suggested, almost desperately. "That's enough to pay you for any risk you think you're taking. There isn't any risk really, I just happen to have taken on a number of responsibilities and I need a good lump sum. Five thousand, on the nail, and it's a deal."

"My original offer stands," Benoni said. "However, Mr. Goldstein is staying at the Dorchester Hotel. If you care to go and see him yourself, he will doubtless be glad to see you. But when he is dealing with someone for the first time, he wants references and absolute assurance that he is buying clean goods. He would wish to see the invoices and the receipts for these jewels, and—but you know how these people work," Benoni went on. "Thank you for giving me the first offer, Mr. Payne."

Payne thought : He's got the money handy, somewhere. The mean devil. And he knows where these came from.

Half an hour ago, Benoni had been his ready market for everything he had, the *open sesame* to his future; now the old man was a deadly danger. He knew the truth all right, and that was the last thing Payne had allowed for. He wasn't really surprised that Benoni was a receiver, but it meant that the police might suspect that. If the police came and questioned him about the Anderson jewels, he might give them a hint, and that would bring them to Richmond Hill

Road; everything would be finished, then. The scraggy hands moved gently over the jewels, as if he were fond of them for what they were as well as for what they were worth.

Payne could see a pile of banknotes in his mind's eye, at least three thousand of them, as much as he could carry comfortably in the case in which he had brought the jewels. It would still be the biggest deal he had ever made, would mean a net profit greater than he usually made in two years, but that wasn't the point. These jewels were worth three times as much, and Benoni would get a big sum from Goldstein. Benoni would take practically no risk, and make as much profit as the man who had taken all the risks.

Let him rot!

"If you change your mind," Payne said, "you know where to find me."

"And if you change yours, I am ready to buy at my price any time this week," Benoni returned courteously. "After that I would have to hold the goods for a longer period, so I would not be able to make the same margin of profit. Thank you again, Mr. Payne." He rolled everything round in a great wad of cotton wool, and put it in the empty case. Payne watched him close the case with slow, deliberate movements.

Payne lifted it off the counter, with an effort.

"Thanks," he said and swung round and went out of the shop. Almost opposite him was the café where he usually had a cup of coffee and a doughnut after a deal with Benoni, but he wanted to get out of the old man's sight. He felt a vicious hatred towards him, felt as if all he wanted to do was get the scraggy neck between his hands and squeeze the life out of him. That would teach the greedy buzzard. Three thousand pounds for all this!

How could he be so sure of himself!

It couldn't be guesswork, but it might be because he knew that Payne had worked at Anderson's shop for a while. Payne felt as if he had been kicked when that thought struck him, for everyone else in the trade would know the same thing, and the moment they thought of Anderson's, they would think of the theft and the murder. He should have kept these goods in hiding for a much longer period, and he would have done if Gwen had not fallen so heavily for that house. He walked towards the Old Bailey, without realising where he was going, weighed down by the case. His car was parked in one of the bombed site car parks in the shadow of St. Paul's.

What the hell was he doing? He ought to get a taxi.

He put the case down and stared along the road; buses, lorries, trucks and cars came along, but no taxis. This was the worst place in London for them. He kept pushing his fingers through his hair. The train of thought which had been interrupted by a realisation of the fact that he was carrying the case, returned. He had to have that house. He was to see the solicitors and the agent tomorrow. He would have to make an additional payment to cover a total of ten per cent of the purchase price—another five hundred and seventy-five pounds. He could do that and still have a few hundred to spare, but he had urged completion quickly, and it was likely to be within three weeks; so at the most he had three weeks to find more money.

How much mortgage could he get on Cornerways?

That wasn't the real question. He had told Gwen and the estate agent that he would put down a total of forty per cent, so he needed—God, he *needed* three thousand almost at once! He had been so sure that he would get six or seven that he had not given a serious thought to the difficulty of finding three.

He couldn't let Gwen down, and he couldn't fool her. She would be present at all the interviews about this, and she was already planning to spend money on the furniture and decorating. If he failed her now, he would never re-cover from it. After all the years of scraping and saving he had justified himself in her eyes, he simply couldn't dis-appoint her again. He couldn't fail Hilda, either, or Maurice.

He had seen the glow of delight in their eyes so vividly, his 'success' had made too deep an impression on them. To disappoint them, to let them down, was unthinkable.

He could get six thousand pounds for everything he had stolen from Anderson's, and—

God!

Old Benoni must know that there was as much to come as he had already been shown. So, he had a good idea how much had been at Anderson's shop. Or had the police found out what had been stolen, and circulated a list? There must have been a copy he had known nothing about. Julian Anderson had probably put one aside, damn him.

An empty taxi slowed down, the driver saw Payne staring blankly ahead of him, and passed by.

"He has that list," Payne said to himself, moving his lips with the words, "and that means everyone else in the trade has it. It's no use going to Goldstein direct, he will have been told to be extra careful. That old swine knows he's got me."

Payne pictured Gwen, examining the curtains and the carpets, which could be bought at valuation. He pictured Hilda, so delighted with this obvious move up the social scale. He pictured Maurice, and seemed to hear him saying: "I knew you'd hit the jackpot one day, Dad." He turned round slowly and walked back to Benoni's shop. He hated the thought of admitting that he was wrong, and of knuckling down to Benoni, but he had to have that money in the bank. He hesitated outside the shop. He saw Benoni inside, peering at him. He clenched his hands and his fists, and wished again that he could choke the life out of the old swine, but that was impossible, yet. The day might come when he could come here and collect what was owing to him—

That was it!

One day, in a few months or a few years, it didn't matter, he would come and take what was owing. He would find out where Benoni kept his ready cash, would study the place as closely as he had studied Anderson's, so that he could repeat the dose. That was it! His eyes began to glisten. He could bring other goods to Benoni from time to time, become the old man's favourite customer, and then one day—

Benoni came to the door, rubbing the palms of his hands together.

"I shouldn't stand there too long, Mr. Payne," he said, his grey eyes narrowed and half hidden by the lids. "I will make my offer in guineas, instead of pounds."

"You're a hell of a tough customer to deal with," Payne said, "but it's a deal."

*   *   *

He took the money away with him, in used one pound and five pound notes. They weighed heavier than the goods he had sold. He was right on top of the world again now, feeling only occasional, momentary twinges of resentment; after all it was simply a matter of getting the full value later. Benoni had almost purred while finishing the deal, there was no doubt that he believed he had got his own way without any trouble. He'd find out!

The second lot of goods was to be delivered tomorrow.

There was still time to catch the bank and deposit the money, Payne realised, but he began to wonder whether it would be wise to put too much cash into the bank at once; the manager would be surprised that he made such a big deposit. He shifted the case from his right hand to his left, twisting round in the hope of seeing a taxi, and, as one came up, realised what he must do. Deposit a thousand, say, and pay a couple of thousand to the house agent against the purchase price of the house. He could wave the receipt in Gwen's face. His heart thumped with the excitement of this prospect, his eyes glowed at the thought of her delight. He settled back in the taxi. He would keep the odd money in his pocket, of course, it would be useful to have a bit of ready cash.

*   *   *

"I've a little surprise for you, sweetie-pie," Payne said. "Guess what it is?"

Gwen stood by the larder, looking round at him. He had never loved her so much. The way she twisted her body round, the way her bosom thrust against her jumper, the gleam in her eyes—God, it was wonderful! And both Maurice and Hilda were out, and would be for the rest of the evening.

"You tell me," she invited.

"A little matter of a receipt," Payne explained, airily. He made a great show of taking the receipt out of his pocket, opening it, and spreading it out before her eyes. As she read, he slid round to her side and put his hand about her. He felt the thumping of her heart, and knew that it was affecting her just as it had him. She turned round, her eyes afire, and thrust herself against him with a passion which carried him back over the years.

*   *   *

About that time, six o'clock on the Monday afternoon, Roger West was sitting at his desk in the little office overlooking the Thames. The crowds streaming over Westminster Bridge were thinning out, but were still in constant movement, and brightened up by the evening sun. The day had been unseasonably warm, the window was down, and he had his coat off and his collar and tie undone. Cope had gone home. Most of the regular daytime staff had, too, but several men were busy finishing off jobs which wouldn't keep. Roger had had a good day. There were no big jobs outstanding, but on his desk was a summary of the Public Prosecutor's case against Julian Anderson, built on all the evidence which he, Roger, had obtained. The longer he studied it, the more it seemed foolproof; if a man were not guilty after such a circumstantial case as this, one could almost give up believing in circumstantial evidence.

He wondered why Julian got under his skin.

He took out his own notes on the case, including oddments

of conversation he had had with Gill—who was now out of London on a job—and Fox. There was nothing new, and, but for the murder of Jennie Campbell, he doubted whether he would have thought twice about Julian's guilt. He knew that Fox had stretched every piece of evidence as far as it could go so as to show that there might be a connection between the two murders, but so far there was absolutely nothing.

He did up his collar and tie, put on his coat, and lit a cigarette and blew smoke out of one side of his mouth. He locked all the papers away, and went out; Big Ben was striking the half hour. It would be seven o'clock before he was home, even if he went straight there. He didn't go straight on, for he saw the door of Fox's little room ajar, and a light shining out. He went in, closing the door quietly behind him. Fox was squinting at some photographs, his thick lips stretched taut over his teeth; it was a pity he had such a simian appearance, it could still hold him back from the final promotion although he had proved that he was a first-class man.

"Hallo, Charley," Roger said. "What've you got?"

"As a matter of fact, Skipper, I think I might have got plenty," Fox said. He put the photographs down, then selected one and handed it to Roger. "What would you say that is?"

Roger studied something which looked like a piece of stone, very bright and shiny on one side; or it might be the broken point of a pin or a needle, magnified several hundred times. It might be a life size piece of quartz. It might be a small stone, magnified half a dozen times.

Fox couldn't wait.

"It's a piece of iron or steel filing, magnified a hundred times," he reported. "I've just had the analyst's report. They took a hell of a time getting it because the fragment was so small, had to send round to some steel manufacturers, but it's worked. That piece is absolutely identical with the filing found on the carpet in Alice Murray's room! Same tensile strength steel, same manufacturer, almost certainly from the same whatever they call it of steel."

"Casting," Roger said. "Or is it forging?"

"Dunno," said Fox, almost shrilly. "Guess where it came from?"

"The rain spots on the floor of the cellar at the Anderson place."

"That's it," squeaked Fox. "That's exactly where it came from. You scraped the dust up from the floor, remember, and said that the rain spots dripping off the coat might have carried something with them. They did, too. This. I've been all over that floor, and there wasn't another speck of the stuff—but by the rainspots, there were five different specks. Whoever opened that safe with a key had been working on steel, turning it, while wearing the shoes and the clothes he wore at the safe. You can tell me I'm jumping to conclusions, but it looks to me as if some of the filings were on his shoes or his clothes when he killed Alice Murray, and some lodged on his coat. The rain washed them out when he went to kill Jennie Campbell. Skipper, we've got a hell of a job on our hands."

Roger grunted.

"Tell you another thing," Fox said. "Julian Anderson's hair's falling out. I've checked closer and strands were found all over the place. We'd better not use that in evidence. We've got a job on all right," he added, and seemed not to know whether to look pleased or sorry.

14

POINTERS

It was half past eleven when Roger got home. There was a light on in the bedroom and one in the hall but no sound anywhere. He went quietly along to the kitchen, and found a piece of pork pie, some cheese and biscuits and two bottles of beer on the table. He put the beer back in the refrigerator, made himself some tea, finished every crumb of food, and went as quietly upstairs. Janet was lying up on the pillows, as if she had tried to keep awake for him but hadn't been able to. He crept about the room, and not until he got into bed beside her did she stir slightly, and make a little grunting noise.

He had been through every possible aspect of the inquiries with Fox, arguing, putting up one argument only to knock it down with another. The whole case was still buzzing through his mind. There had been another man that night at Alice Murray's: the cyclist. There had been the other boy friend; the middle-aged man. He still hadn't been found, and he must have been extraordinarily careful, because no one except Jennifer Ling seemed to have set eyes on him—and she could not add anything to what she had already said.

There was nothing at all to work on where Jennie Campbell was concerned.

Roger dropped off thinking about the mystery, and woke with a start in broad daylight, with Scoopy standing by the side of the bed with a tea tray in his hands and Janet stirring by his side. Richard was somewhere upstairs, whistling.

"It's nearly half past seven so I thought you ought to be up," Scoopy said. "I hope you weren't in very late last night, Dad."

"Not really late," Roger mumbled. "My, that tea looks good!" He hitched himself up, as Scoopy put the tray on the bedside table, and Janet murmured. "It *can't* be morning already."

"It is, Mum," Scoopy said. "Nearly half past seven."

"There must be something you want very badly, or you wouldn't be up, washed, hair brushed and the tea made," Janet said, sitting upright at last. "What is it, Tyke?"

"Oh, nothing much," Scoopy said airily. "Only at seven o'clock, that girl called again."

"That *girl*?" asked Roger.

"The one who called last night."

"You know," Richard contributed from the door. He came sauntering in, red striped pyjama jacket wide open, hair very wet, eyes a little heavy from catarrh. "The one we left the note about."

"I don't get this," Roger said.

"Surely—" Janet began, and added in exasperation: "You boys are absolutely impossible! Why don't you *ever* think what you're doing? I told you to write a note and tell your father about Miss Ling, and you must have forgotten."

"But I didn't!" exclaimed Scoopy. "I wrote it."

"And I put it under the bottles on the table," Richard said hotly.

"Good lord!" exclaimed Roger. "I didn't have any beer, and put the bottles straight back in the frig. This must have stuck to the bottom. But what—"

"It couldn't have been bigger than a postage stamp, then," Janet said, tartly.

"Well, the paper was a bit small," Scoopy admitted. "But—"

"What's it all about, anyhow?" asked Roger eagerly. "Miss Ling. *Jennifer* Ling?" His voice rose.

"Yes, that's right. She lives at 24, Manville Street. Apparently you interviewed her about that other girl's murder," Janet told him. "She wants to talk to you some time before eight o'clock this morning. She's going to Paris, modelling for a photographer, and—"

"Get me my clothes!" Roger said, urgently. "Scoop, run round to Miss Ling's flat and tell her I'm on my way. Don't let her leave." He thrust his feet out of bed, Scoopy darted to one side, and Roger hurried to the bathroom. Nine minutes level from the time he had heard about the Ling girl's call he was putting down an empty tea cup, and saying to Janet: "I'll be back in half an hour." It was ten minutes to eight when he reached 24, Manville Street. Outside it was Ted's antiquated M.G., with a suitcase in the back, and Scoopy standing as if on guard.

"She obviously hasn't left yet, so I didn't go in," he said.

"Nice work," said Roger. "Thanks, old chap." He hurried into the house, the front door of which was ajar, and up the stairs. The appetising smell of frying bacon teased him again; this girl certainly liked her food. The door of the flatlet was ajar, too, and Ted was looking out. As soon as he caught sight of Roger he called out to the girl, who was not in sight.

Ted opened the door wider saying: "Come in, sir. Jenny's got some hot news for you." He looked only about Scoopy's age as he grinned, and the girl, dressed this morning in a vivid blue coat and skirt, wearing a dashing little hat, looking slim, lovely and provocative with a small apron tied round her waist, appeared from the kitchen.

"Thank goodness you've come," she welcomed. "I was going to try to pass on the message through Ted, but he *never* gets messages straight."

"Thank you, ma'am."

"Well, you don't. Mr. West, I've seen the man who was in Alice Murray's room. I saw him last night," Jennifer Ling announced.

Roger thought: Well, well, here's the big break at last. Aloud, he asked eagerly: "Are you sure?"

"Positive. I saw him from the same kind of angle again." She spoke with absolute certainty. "I was on top of a bus, coming home from the West End, and he was walking along the street. He'd just come out of a shop in King's Road, not far from the Chelsea Town Hall. I nearly fell off the bus to catch up with him, but he turned down a street just past the Town Hall, and I think I saw him getting into a car as the bus passed the end of the street. Anyhow, I lost him."

"Too bad," said Roger, and groaned at the lost time and the lost chance. "What was he wearing?"

"Oh, just a suit," Jennifer answered, "and he was carrying a hat. It was something about the way he walked which made me so certain. He had rather nice hair, turning to grey a little, and with some waves at the side. I did just catch a glimpse of his profile, and it was that which made me positive. It was—well, how *do* you describe a kind of angle profile? Ted!" She stepped across to her fiancé, put her fingers up to his chin, and said: "Turn your head a little that way." Ted obliged. "A bit more," Jennifer ordered, and when Ted was standing to her satisfaction, she went on to Roger: "If you stand where I am now, you'll see what I mean. I could just make out his cheekbone, and his forehead, and the tip of his nose."

That meant she had seen enough for her evidence to be valuable.

"How long are you going to be away for?" Roger asked.

"Oh, only four days—it's my first professional trip abroad, I'm *wildly* excited. Ted, what's the time?"

It was five past eight.

*   *   *

There were about thirty shops in the parade near the Town Hall, and Jennifer Ling could not be sure which one the man had come out of. Roger pulled up outside a bank, on a corner, and left his car. As he reached the other side of the road, Fox and two other Yard sergeants arrived in a car which pulled up just round the corner. Roger had briefed them from home, but had a word with them before they began to question the shopkeepers.

"He's six feet two, greying hair, sometimes carries his hat, a trilby, wears well-cut clothes, aged probably in the middle forties. He was in one of these shops at about five o'clock yesterday afternoon, started to walk from them towards the Town Hall, and had his car parked round the first corner beyond the Town Hall." Roger saw two more big men hurrying up, both from the Division. "Give them the details, Charley," he ordered. "The Division ought to have a look for that car." He had a word with the two Divisional men, and then went to the end shop on the parade; a tobacconist and confectioner. He drew a blank from a man who seemed to know what he was talking about. A men's outfitters and a greengrocer's yielded nothing at all, but they might if they were questioned more closely. He saw Fox go into an estate agent's, the one whose board was still up at Cornerways, with a great red SOLD nailed across it. He went into a butcher's shop, and came out immediately; the shop had closed at midday on the Monday, so the man hadn't gone in there. Then he saw Fox dart out of the agent's, obviously looking for him, and as excited as a monkey who had found an unexpected source of bananas.

"Skipper!" he called, and made several people glance round. He drew up. "We've scored a bull! There was a chap in here at a quarter to five last night, he's just bought a house and paid some money down on it—a couple of thousand, in cash. He fits that Ling girl's description perfectly, and we've got his name, address, the lot. A Mr. John Payne."

*　　*　　*

"John *Payne*," gasped old Clayton. "Why, a John Payne, he was usually called Jack, used to work here. He left about five years ago."

*　　*　　*

"Now we're really on the move," Fox said with deep satisfaction. "This one is too perfect to be wrong, isn't it,

Skipper? Payne's a working jeweller, runs his own little business, buys and sells all over the south of England, even has his own workshop, with a lathe and a little smelting furnace. What are you going to do? Have a talk with him first, or find out what you can about him before interviewing him?"

"We want all the information we can get before we do anything," Roger answered. "He's been pretty smart, and he may have an alibi for the murders. Let's find him, have him watched, and try to find out where he was on the two nights that matter before we talk to him. Like to handle that yourself?"

"Just give me a chance!"

"You've got your chance," Roger said. "Keep me posted with every development, no matter how small it is. If you'd like me to be sententious, make a note of this: two heads are better than one and four eyes are better than two."

"Many hands make light work," grinned Fox, "and then there's that one about too many cooks! What we could really do with is a peek into Payne's workshop."

"Only with a search warrant."

"Of course, I'm an officer of the law," said Fox, virtuously. "I'll settle for some fingerprints. Damned queer thing they're planning to buy a house in Bell Street, isn't it? Now that *is* a coincidence for you."

"Yes," Roger said, expressionlessly.

He arranged for Fox to have two detective officers to help him, and then went on to the Yard. It was beginning to look as if there would soon be a break in the case, but there was another angle of it which he did not like at all. He looked in at his Bell Street house twice that day, and each time Scoopy or Richard made some comment about the Payne girl. Janet was now finding it amusing. Roger checked during the day, found out what time Hilda Payne left her work, and then checked with Janet, who told him that the Payne family were due to visit Cornerways again at half

past six that evening. Roger made a point of being home
by twenty past six.

Janet was out, probably with a neighbour. The boys were
doing their cycling circus act farther down the street, and
it was no coincidence that they were outside Cornerways.
Roger stayed in the front room, watching the street, and
saw Payne's old Austin pass the window. He went out into
the garden. It was still quite light, although electric lamps
would soon be needed indoors. He had left his car outside,
deliberately, now he put up the bonnet and pretended to
tinker with the plugs, but he watched the people getting out
of the Austin. The woman came first, and she was as striking
as Mrs. Montifiore had said, in a bold, rather flamboyant
way. There was a natural gaiety about her, too. Roger had
a sense not only of physical well-being and attractiveness,
but of vitality. The girl climbed out next. Scoopy was watching her very closely, and the first thing she did was to look
across the road and wave; Scoopy waved back.

Then Payne got out.

He fitted the Ling girl's description perfectly, and the
moment he moved, carrying his hat, Roger realised exactly
why the girl had been so sure.

The family went into Cornerways.

They left a little after half past seven, followed by Charley
Fox, who would work night and day if he thought it would
bring results. Roger was in the kitchen by then, Janet was
home, and the boys were helping to lay supper and at the
same time watching television. At supper, it was easy to turn
the subject to Cornerways; Janet seemed to have lost her
resentment.

"Mrs. Montifiore says that she doesn't like Payne much,"
Scoopy volunteered, "but she thinks Mrs. Payne and the
girl—er, her name's Hilda, Dad—are very nice. She says
Payne talks too big, and he rather looks as if he would, Dad,
doesn't he?"

"Does he?"

"I saw you watching him," Scoopy declared knowingly.

"You'll have to leave school and become a policeman," Roger chaffed. "Think Payne looks too big-headed, Fish?"

"Well, I don't know," answered Richard, with great concentration. "I don't exactly *like* any of them."

"Don't be ridiculous," Janet said, absently. "You don't know them, and you can't like or dislike people you don't know. Mrs. Monty says that they seem an absolutely devoted family, that's one good thing. There's a boy, named Maurice, about Scoop's age."

"I say!" exclaimed Scoopy. "We'll soon get an excuse to meet them, then. Fish and I can always scrape up an acquaintance with another chap." His eyes glowed. "I wonder what Payne does for a living."

"He can't be much," declared Richard, scornfully. "Otherwise he wouldn't go about in that old Austin. You should hear the engine knocking, Dad."

Roger didn't speak.

Quite out of the blue, Scoopy looked across at him, glanced down at some bread and butter on which he was spreading raspberry jam, and asked quietly:

"Dad, was it an accident, do you think, or did you know that one of your Scotland Yard chaps came into the street just after the Paynes, and followed them when they left? I couldn't help noticing. I wouldn't have known, but I saw the man one day last winter, when you had someone show us round the Yard."

Richard's eyes were glowing.

Roger said: "If it wasn't a coincidence, I'll soon find out about it, but I don't know everything that goes on at the Yard, you know."

"You know most things," Richard remarked confidently. "I say, Dad, he's not a *crook* is he?"

"Richard!" exclaimed Janet.

Roger said reasoningly: "Now this is the kind of loose talk which mustn't go any farther, chaps. You can talk like it round the table and among the family, but keep it absolutely dark with anyone else. That clear, Fish?"

"Yes, Dad. Absolutely. Black as pitch."

Scoopy was sitting very still, and staring down at the bread and butter; the jam was spread thinly, but he had not put any into his mouth. He had become very straight-faced, all hint of a smile gone. Janet watched him, and Roger shook his head at her. Slowly, Scoopy began to eat, but it was some time before he joined in the conversation.

*   *   *

"*Is* there something funny about the Paynes?" Janet asked, when the boys had gone out to a special evening at their youth club, which had a well equipped gymnasium; Scoopy especially was keen on physical training, and was a boxer of exceptional promise.

"Yes," answered Roger, "but I'm not sure how funny, yet. What time will the boys be back?"

"About eleven," Janet said. "Why?"

"Just wondered," responded Roger, airily.

Janet laughed . . .

She would have been far less contented and compliant had she known that the boys had not gone to the club . . .

They were cycling fast up Putney High Street towards Richmond Hill Road. There was little traffic about, their three-speed gears were working well, and the hill called for no special effort. Once in Richmond Hill Road they were able to cycle two abreast for a few minutes, and Richard said eagerly:

"If there's a Yard man watching, then there's not much doubt, is there?"

"Shouldn't think so," agreed Scoopy. "I hope to heaven there isn't. I'd hate to think that girl—"

He didn't finish, and Richard did not taunt him. Obviously he understood that some deep compulsion drove his brother into trying to find out the truth about the Paynes. They felt nearly sure of the truth, a little later, for they saw Fox's car parked on the small driveway of an empty house—not quite opposite the Payne's house. This driveway was heaven-sent to Fox, for there were a lot of thick shrubs bordering it, and plenty of places to hide while watching Payne's place.

In his heart, Charley Fox felt quite sure how 'funny' Payne was, and he had only one urgent desire: to look in the workshop at the back of the man's garage. He had built up a complete dossier on the man, he knew about his visits to old Benoni, who had long been suspected of acting as a fence. He knew that Benoni had recently made a big sale to an American buyer, named Aaron Goldstein, and that Goldstein had an unblemished reputation. A request for a close inspection of jewellery he had with him en route for New York was on its way to Police Headquarters. Fox was drawing up a case which looked to him—and to Roger—almost unassailable.

They now knew, for instance, that Payne had been out on the night of Alice Murray's murder, and that he had used his son's bicycle. A policeman on his beat had noticed him with the bicycle, and thought idly that his car must be laid up. The same policeman was able to say that Payne had been out in his car on the night of the murder of Jennie Campbell. But Fox wanted more than this, and believed that he could get it at the workshop without much difficulty. This workshop was behind Payne's garage, and practically an extension to it. There was a side door, near the house. Fox made it his job to watch the little house in Richmond Hill Road, with one other man. They kept a complete time-table of Payne's movements, as well as those of the family. It was remarkable that for the first four days there was no time of the day or night when the house was really empty; either the boy, the girl, or one or the other of the parents was there all the time. Fox saw a lot of Gwen Payne, and got exactly the same impression of her as Roger had.

It was Friday evening, just after dark, when all four of them left the house together in the Austin. Fox was on duty, watching from along the road. He heard them laughing and talking gaily, and told himself that there was no need to

think that Payne suspected he was being watched; the longer
that state of ignorance lasted, the better. Fox waited for ten
minutes, and then went across the road. He could not be
sure that the family was out for the evening, but thought
it likely. He stepped into the garage, the front of which had
been left open. The door which led to the side of the house
was ajar, but another, presumably leading to the workshop,
was closed and locked. Fox stepped towards the house, and
in the back garden saw the workshop at close quarters for
the first time. There was frosted glass in the lower panes of
the windows, to make sure that no one could look in. They
were small windows, too. He tried the workshop door again,
and longed to force it. He went to the front of the garage,
closed the doors, and used his torch to try to find something
which he could take away, and on which there might be
fingerprints.

He found exactly what he wanted, and his heart began to
beat fast, for this was a box of chocolates, of the same brand
as those found in Alice Murray's flat. He shone the torch
on the shiny surface, and saw fingerprints, but they were not
clear enough for him even to guess at the pattern after
a close scrutiny with the naked eye. He wrapped the box
carefully in a sheet of plastic, slid it into his pocket, and
turned towards the garage doors. The street lighting was so
dark that he did not think there was any serious risk of being
seen or recognised. He pushed one of the double doors open,
so as to leave them exactly as he had found them, and it
scraped against the cement of the driveway. He had to push
hard.

He was pushing when he was struck savagely on the back
of the head by a man he did not even see.

15

FEAR

PAYNE struck the little man twice, each time savagely, heard him gasp, and saw him falling. He stopped him, took his weight, and dragged him farther into the garage. A car passed with its headlights on and dipped, but no one else appeared. He went to the door and pulled it to again, then put on the light. It shone on the ugly man's face, the thick slack lips. There was a trickle of blood on his right temple. Payne knelt down beside him and felt his pulse; it seemed quite steady. Payne himself was breathing very heavily. He lit a cigarette, and fought against the temptation to go indoors and get himself a drink.

He had realised that he was being followed for the past few days, and had seen men going in and out of the garden of the empty house across the road, as well as following him in a car now and again. He had known real fear almost for the first time, and one thing had been vital: to find out who the men were. One was a little, ugly chap, surely too small to be a policeman. That was Payne's chief hope.

Payne had arranged to take Gwen and the children to a picture palace, and leave them there. He had stayed away from the house long enough to allow the man to go snooping, and the tactics had worked perfectly. But now that he had the man at his feet, he did not know what to do.

He spread the coat wide, dipped into the inside pocket, found a shiny leather wallet, and took it out. He was almost too frightened to open it, for fear of what he might find; he had never felt like this before. His teeth were clamped together when he opened the wallet, took out some cards including a driving licence, saw that the man had several five pound notes with him—and then found a card which looked very different from the rest. He gulped, and carried it close to the light.

There it was: *Detective Sergeant Charles Fox, Criminal Investigation Department, New Scotland Yard, S.W.1.*

Payne moaned, sotto voce: *"Oh, God, oh God."* At least there was only one of them—he had never seen two together, just one at a time.

There was still hope.

The man on the floor did not stir. The trickle of blood was much thicker. Payne stood up, unlocked the workshop door and switched on the bright light, then came back and lifted the man up; he was unexpectedly heavy. Payne stretched him out on an old bench, used for the garden in the summer, and filled a jug with water, hesitated, and then let it fall slowly on to the man's face. Almost at once there was a reaction; the eyes screwed up, the nose and lips twitched. Payne poured more freely, and Fox gasped.

He opened his eyes.

Payne said: "Don't move and don't shout. This place is soundproof."

Small bright eyes in the monkeylike face were staring at him intently. He wanted to strike the man just for the sake of hurting, but kept his hands by his side, and fought to breathe evenly. He saw that the water had mixed with the blood, thinning it, so that now the whole of one side of the man's face was tinged pink.

"Who else knows you're on to me?" he demanded.

He thought: If I'm wrong about the other man, I'll be all right. If he's doing this off his own bat, I can put him away, and there'll be nothing to worry about. He seemed to hear his own voice in the thoughts, and deep down within him he knew that he was deceiving himself.

He gripped the man's shoulder, and shook vigorously.

"Come on, tell me who else knows you're on to me?"

The man's lips moved, and he said very huskily:

"Everyone at the Yard."

"That's a lie!"

"What makes you think I would lie to you?" the man asked weakly. What was his name? Fox, yes, that was right, Fox. "The whole Department's after you, Payne. You'll only make it worse for yourself if you don't let me go."

Payne said, savagely: "That's a lie and you know it. You've come snooping by yourself, haven't you? Policemen don't hunt in ones, they hunt in pairs. You're just following a hunch, you're in this by yourself. Come on, admit it."

"If I don't report back by twelve o'clock, they'll send a Squad car here." Fox's voice was a little stronger.

Payne said, thinly: "We'll see about that, we'll wait until twelve o'clock."

There was no way to be sure, but he believed that the other was lying; he thought he saw the fear in his eyes. He himself felt better. He raised the man's head and pressed roughly, felt him wince, but satisfied himself that the skull wasn't seriously damaged. He let the head fall, quite gently, picked up an old raincoat—the one he had used for the Anderson raid, and which he used when working in here if it were cold—and bundled it up into a rough pillow.

"Make a sound, and I'll gum your lips up," he threatened. "Just answer my questions. Who put you on to me?"

Fox spoke in the stronger, husky voice. "There are hundreds of detectives at the Yard. Hundreds of them. When we want a killer, we put every man we've got on to hunting for him. We question everyone who might be able to help. We spend weeks, even months concentrating on the job, and sooner or later something cracks. You were seen at Alice Murray's place the night you killed her—and seen coming out of that estate agent's yesterday. That's how we got on to you."

Payne thought: God! Because of that bloody house!

Then he thought: *What will Gwen say?*

The question terrified him, driving him near to a frenzy of panic. He had left her so happy—the children, too. He had hidden his private fears from them, he was sure that none of them had the slightest idea that he had been watched and followed.

They must never know.

Fox said, in his husky, matter-of-fact way :

"You'll only make it worse for yourself if you don't give yourself up, Payne. Let me take you in, and I'll make it as easy as I can for you." When Payne didn't answer, he went on : "If you're co-operative it can make a lot of difference, but if you leave me here and go on the run, you'll be hunted down like a beast. Ever thought what that would be like? You'd be afraid of being seen anywhere, and you'd always be on the move. You'd be hungry and thirsty all the time."

Payne still didn't speak.

"Every newspaper would have your photograph and they'd build it up," Fox went on. "You know that, Payne. You'd get ten times as much newspaper space if you run for it, especially if you injure me."

He did not seem in any way frightened, but watched Payne closely. Payne followed everything he said while his own thoughts were darting to and fro.

"It will be far worse for your wife and family," Fox continued. "I've seen quite a lot of them in the past few days. They're nice people. Imagine what it would be like if every time they opened a newspaper they saw your photograph— probably saw pictures of the bloodhounds after you. What do you think it would do to them, Payne? It would be bad enough if they come back tonight and found you'd been taken to the Yard, but Superintendent West would be here, he'd break it to them. He'd make it just as easy as he could, and he would for you, too. But if you don't let me take you along, it will be hell for them. You're not going to send them to hell, are you, Payne?"

Payne lashed out, striking him three times in the face, each a savage, agonising blow. Fox gasped with pain, and drew in a shuddering breath, his whole body hunched up as if to help fend off another attack.

Standing over him, glaring, Payne said thickly :

"Don't talk about my family again. Understand that? Don't talk about them. They're not going to know. They'll never know."

Fox felt blood trickling into his mouth from his nose, and his jaw felt as if it were broken, but the way Payne spoke and the significance of what he said slashed through the pain.

"What the devil——" he began.

"*I told you to shut up!*" Payne rasped, and struck him again, a cruel blow on the mouth. "They're never going to know." He began to look about him, and was breathing hissingly through parted lips. "I can't do that to them, I can't let them down," he said. "They're never going to know."

"Listen, Payne," Fox made himself say. He found it almost impossible to get words out, his mouth was so painful, and his lips were already swelling. "You don't know what you're saying. The Yard will catch up with you whatever you do to me. They'll have to know."

"They're never going to know," Payne breathed. "And you're not going to get me. I wasn't born to be hanged." He took in a shuddering breath, then looked about him wildly, snatched up some of the wadding in which jewellery was wrapped, and stuffed a wadge into Fox's mouth. Fox tried to spit it out, and on the instant it was stained with blood, but Payne rammed it in. Fox began to cough and choke. Payne was muttering to himself all the time—while he snatched up a piece of rope and bound the other's ankles, found a smaller piece and bound his wrists. Fox edged himself desperately to one side, still choking and coughing, trying desperately to breathe through his nostrils. He could see only a moving blur, and knew what Payne was doing but he could not help himself.

Payne stood back from him.

"I hope you rot," he said, savagely, and then he raised his hands and stared at the little gas burner beneath the furnace for melting down the silver and gold. He began to grin, a slashing, evil grin, and there was actually laughter in his eyes. "You'll rot all right. You've done all the harm you'll ever do!" He stretched across Fox, and turned on the gas tap; the gas began to hiss. "Hear that? That's gas, that'll kill you, you won't last for half an hour. The workshop's almost sealed up, see, I made sure that no one could sneak up on me." He thrust his face forward in an animal gloating, and then he backed towards the door. He saw Fox raise his head, saw the glint in the man's eyes, and knew that he understood.

He went out, slammed the door, and locked it. He did not think twice about the killing, murder seemed part of his life; he had *wanted* to kill Fox.

* * *

Across the road, Martin called Scoopy and Richard called Richard West, were standing just in sight of the garage and the small semi-detached house. They had arrived nearly half an hour before, parked their cycles some distance away, and gone into the garden of the empty house after Fox had left for Payne's garage. They had seen a little, but were not sure exactly what had happened. When Fox—the man whom Martin had recognised from the Yard—had gone into the garage, they had felt a thrill of excitement tinged on Martin's side with a kind of despair; everything seemed to be so obvious now, and the man Payne was a crook.

Martin kept seeing the daughter in his mind's eye.

He had never felt like this about a girl before. He had noticed the prettier ones, and gone into slightly sheepish or over-hilarious detail about vital statistics with other boys, and felt an occasional stirring of interest, but never had a girl made such an impression on him as Hilda Payne. It had happened almost the first moment he had set eyes on her, when she had got out of the little Austin, stood up, and looked straight at him. His heart had begun to beat very fast with a most unfamiliar excitement, and that had continued. He felt as if he were transported out of his everyday world to a new one which promised fresh understanding and delights.

For the first time in his sixteen years, he had gone to bed obsessed by a girl, had lain awake for an hour or more thinking of her, and had woken with the thought of her vivid on his mind. It had not faded, as he knew that his mother hoped and his father thought it would. He found himself making excuses to watch Cornerways, in case Hilda—he had learned the name from Mrs. Montifiore—called again. He kept reminding himself that Mrs. Montifiore had told him that the Paynes hoped to move in during the Spring— say, in a month's time. He already knew the girl, so there would be no need to waste time scraping an acquaintance. In fact the very next time she came, he had decided, he would go across and speak to her. He could tell that she liked him; and he had never seen anyone with that kind of half smile before—rather as if she were inviting him to come and talk to her.

Then, he had recognised Fox.

When he had realised the truth, it had almost frightened him.

He did not care at all about Payne, no one who had met the man took to him, but Hilda—what would happen to her if her father was proved to be a crook? What chance had he, the son of a C.I.D. superintendent, of becoming friendly with the daughter of a man who was in prison? It was all very well thinking that the girl wasn't responsible for her father, but—what would people say? What would the neighbours of Bell Street do, for instance?

Even if Hilda and her mother and brother came, it would be impossible for them to settle in a new neighbourhood when everyone knew the truth. He, Martin West, wouldn't care what people said, wouldn't care what his own mother or father said, but—how many others would be helpful and understanding?

He felt that he had to find out the truth, and Richard had not hesitated to say 'yes' when he had suggested coming here to see if Fox or other men from Scotland Yard were watching Payne's house. If they were, it implied that they believed Payne guilty of a serious crime.

After Fox had gone into the garage, Payne had driven up in his Austin, and gone past the approach to the garage, then walked back. That in itself had been surprising; why hadn't he pulled up right outside his own house even if he didn't want to drive in? The boys had seen him approach the garage on foot, but were too far away to notice anything, or see what happened, but they saw the garage doors close.

Richard said: "What are we going to do, Scoop?"

"I don't know," Martin had to admit.

"Do you think that Yard chap is all right?"

"He can look after himself, take it from me," Martin said. "All of these chaps are thoroughly well trained in judo and all kinds of tricks. I expect he's questioning Payne."

"I suppose so," Richard conceded, and then he added more brightly: "Yes, I bet that's it! Scoop, I bet I see exactly what's happened! I'll bet Payne knew the Yard man was coming to question him, and didn't want his wife or the family to hear so he arranged to meet the Yard man here when they'd gone out. That all adds up, doesn't it?"

Martin said, slowly: "Yes, I suppose it does."

"Well, it was your idea!" Richard spoke with urgent eagerness. "I only elaborated it, but when you come to think, it makes sense. I mean, look how often Dad goes and talks to people when he simply wants to get information from them. He says that a quiet chat, when no one else can overhear and the man you're questioning isn't worried about what his friends or his family will think, often does a world of good. And he says it's surprising how often a suspect *isn't* the crook."

Martin said, more brightly: "Yes, so he does."

"If you ask me, this man from the Yard is having it out with Payne," went on Richard. "They may be there for a long time yet. I wouldn't be surprised if they don't go into the house, soon. And I wouldn't be surprised if this isn't one of those cases where the wrong man is being suspected. After all, Dad didn't seem to know anything about it, and if it were a big case, he would know something."

"I thought he snapped a bit," Martin observed, thoughtfully, "as if he didn't want us to know what he knew. But I daresay you're right. It's dark enough now, let's go a bit closer. You game?"

"You just try to keep me away!"

They moved their bicycles to the garden of the empty house, and walked towards Payne's place on the opposite side of the road. As they drew level, they heard a door slam, and two men say something. Then a glow of light which appeared to come from the back of the garage was shut out. Soon there were footsteps, and another door slammed.

"There you are!" Richard said triumphantly. "They've gone into the house."

"I only heard one pair of footsteps," Martin objected.

"Oh, you're just being difficult. How could you be sure? It's only a step, and the door made a hell of a lot of noise, anyhow. Look! A light's gone on. I wouldn't mind betting they've gone over there to have a drink, they're probably the best of friends by now. Scoop, don't you think we ought to go back? If we get to the club late, no one will ask us any questions, but if we don't go at all we can't *lie* to Mum and Dad."

Martin didn't answer.

"Scoop, don't stand there like a stuffed dummy! We ought to put in an appearance, if nothing else. It must be well after eight o'clock, and—"

"Tell you what," Scoopy interrupted, with an elder brother's authority, "you go to the club and give my apologies, and then go home at the usual time. If I'm not there, tell Dad where I am. Then I'll be able to hang about and see Hilda—Hilda Payne." In the dim street light, he looked at his brother appealingly, as if he were pleading not to be called crazy. They stood quietly for what seemed a long time, with a few cars passing, and two buses thundering along in this straight stretch of road.

Then Richard said abruptly: "All right, Scoop."

"*Thanks*, old chap!"

"I can imagine what it's like if you feel like that about a girl," Richard said, with earnest understanding. "I hope everything works out all right, Scoop." He seemed a little overcome, and turned and strode away; two minutes later, Martin saw him wheeling his bicycle out of the garden, saw the lights go on, and watched the red lamp fading in the distance.

Good old Fish!

Now, Martin crossed the road, and went cautiously into Payne's garage.

16

LIKE FATHER LIKE SON

MARTIN stood in the darkness of the garage for half a minute, his heart thumping with an unfamiliar kind of emotion. He felt as if he were choking. There was only a sliver of light from the garage doors, which had not been tightly closed and for that half minute he could make out nothing but the vague shape of the window, on his right. Then he began to pick out oddments; dark round shapes hanging on the pale coloured walls, for instance—some old tyres. He moved cautiously, and kicked against something which gave out a loud clang; it made him stop abruptly. No one seemed to have heard. He moved back towards the doors, where the light switch was likely to be, and longed for a torch; the frustrating thing was that Richard always carried one, but he seldom troubled to. He groped for the switch, found it, kept its position in mind, and then went to the doors and closed them more tightly. When the light was on, it wouldn't be seen so easily from the street or from the house.

He switched on the light.

It was a small garage, smelly with oil, with only just room for a car, and the only surprising thing was a door at the back and a door at the side. He went towards these. The side door was unlocked, and when he opened it a few inches and peered through, he saw that there was a light on at the back of the house but none at the side. He closed the door quickly, then turned to the one in the end wall of the garage.

This was locked.

It seemed more solid than the side door, too, and made no noise when he pressed against it. There was no point in pushing for the sake of pushing, so he drew back, then put out the light, for there was a switch at this end. He crept out by the side door and saw the light still on at the back of the house. He had a strangely guilty feeling, as well as one of fear, as he crept towards the back door, where light shone through glass panels. He reached the window, and looked in cautiously. No one was in the kitchen, but another light was on in a passage leading off it. That was a relief; Fox and Payne must have gone to the front of the house. Probably they were sitting back and having a drink; Richard was almost certainly right.

But at least he could look round here while he was about it, Martin decided.

The kitchen light showed a section of the garage which had two high windows. It was about six feet long by ten feet or so, and in complete darkness. There were clouds tonight, so the sky was darker than usual, too. Scoopy tiptoed to try to see through the windows, but could not; the windows' bottom sections were frosted, anyhow, but the top seemed clear. He jumped up once or twice but could not get high enough; then he stretched up, gripped the narrow window ledge, and began to haul himself up by his arms. With a little better purchase it would have been easy, because he was used to this kind of exercise in the gymnasium, but now he was hanging on by the tips of his fingers, and could not be sure he would make it. Gradually, muscles strained and neck feeling tight and constricted, he hauled himself up until his eyes were on a level with the top, and the plain glass of the window.

He could not see a thing; it was pitch dark inside.

"Oh, what's the use!" he muttered in vexation, and prepared himself for the drop, then let go. He judged it well, his knees bent, and he leaned against the back of the shed for a few moments, wondering what to do next. He smelt something—rather like gas—but did not give that any thought. There were often smells about a garage or a workshop.

He stood quite still, frowning, trying to think.

Obviously, this *was* some kind of a workshop—a tool-shed, perhaps. A lot of people were fussy about their tools, and he knew that old Mr. Montifiore, for instance, had a special padlock on the door of his tool-shed, but this was different; anyone could see in, because light was wanted for work at the bench inside the shed.

Was there anything in this workshop or whatever-it-was to explain what Payne did for a living? Had the Yard man come in here, for instance, and looked round before going to the house itself?

Had he really gone to the house?

Years of listening to his father talking, hearing a hundred examples of detailed deductive reasoning, had taught Martin a great deal, and much of it he did not realise that he knew. Now he was asking himself the kind of questions which his father would ask. He was remembering how often his father had said that when one heard a thing, one seldom listened properly. There were often three or four sounds when a listener noticed only one or two. The power of observation was the most important single factor in detection, the second was to have a trained and retentive memory. Now, Scoopy found himself thinking back to the slamming of the door. What would that tell his father? A door might slam in the wind, but there was no wind tonight. So, it had either been pulled too sharply by accident, or slammed in a temper.

There were the footsteps, too.

Scoopy made himself stand quite still, and think back to the moment. First, the door had slammed—and there had been a little rattle of metal!—he had forgotten that. Oh, yes, and one of the men had spoken: it had just been a word or two, quite indistinguishable, but also quite definite; now Scoopy told himself that it was the kind of expletive which someone would use in anger.

Why in anger, tonight?

There had been the footsteps; four or five. Well, which was it? Four or five? He tried to remember vividly enough to count. One—two—three—four, all sharp footsteps, the kind made by steel heel protectors on hard ground, such as cement or stone, and then a softer one, the kind of sound that might come when one stepped on a stair—the back doorstep, of course! *One—two—three—four—up on the ball of his foot!* That was it. Now that he could recall everything so vividly, Scoopy was quite sure of one thing: there had only been one man.

So, where was the Yard detective?

There was only one possible place, Scoopy reasoned, and turned round and stared at the dark wall of the workshop: in there. His heart was hammering, his mind worked very quickly, going backwards and forwards over events remembering the scraping of the garage door, the silence, the fact that there had been no sound until that door had slammed. There was no doubt that the Yard man had gone into the garage but not come out. If he had come out of the side door on to that hard ground between the garage and the back door he, Martin, would have heard something; and Richard would have, for certain.

How far away was he from a telephone, or from a police call box?

Scoopy did not know this road well. He did know that in a few minutes he could be on his bicycle, within five he could make a call to 999, and have the police at this spot within ten minutes. That was the obvious thing to do, *if* he could be sure that there was any need for it. But supposing there was not? Supposing he had reasoned wrongly—even supposing he had been preoccupied, and not heard the Yard man moving from the garage to the house. He couldn't be sure that there was any need for an emergency call, and what a fool he would look if he brought the police out here for no reason at all.

Another thought slipped into his mind.

There might be good reason for *not* bringing the police here. If Payne was being watched, for instance, even if he had been questioned tonight, there was a possibility that the Yard was not yet ready to act; that was another thing his father was very strong on: never being too hasty. "More good cases are spoilt by impetuous action than any other single factor; before an arrest is made a case must be fool-proof."

Well, this wasn't anywhere near foolproof.

Scoopy pushed his fingers through his straight hair, and was surprised that his forehead was so wet with sweat. He moved a little way from the side of the shed or workshop, knowing that there was only one thing he could possibly do : make absolutely sure that there was something wrong. It was easy, really, he simply had to break that glass and look inside.

If only he had a torch.

There might be one in the garage !

He hurried to the side door, warning himself to be very careful; at least his rubber soled shoes made no sound. He opened the door, stepped in and switched on the light, then looked about the window ledge and some old boxes where tools were standing; he saw no sign of a torch. When you came to think, there was hardly any need for one in the garage with a light switch at either end. He scowled in disappointment, then turned and studied the heavier door, touched the handle and pushed again, but there was no hope of getting inside. There was a Yale lock; Payne certainly made sure that no one could get in easily. Scoopy put his shoulder to the door and heaved, but apart from making a dull booming noise, which he did not want, there was no result. Despondently, he turned round again.

Then he saw a box of matches.

His heart leapt.

It looked an old, often used box of the kind in which screws or washers might be kept, and his heart was in his mouth when he picked it up and shook it. The light rattling sound of matches rewarded him. He opened the box, and saw at least a dozen red-headed matches, the kind that would strike on any rough surface; he did not need the box ! He slipped it into his pocket, then eyed one of the old wooden boxes.

"Just what I want," he said aloud.

He took the tools off it, carefully, put them on the window ledge, and lifted the box; it was quite heavy and solid. He put out the light and, with extreme care, carried the box out, keeping the door open with his foot to make sure it didn't bang. At last, the door was safely and silently closed, and he was close to the window with the wooden box. He pushed it a little nearer. He was breathing very hard, but excitement had quite overcome fear. He glanced round at the house, where the light was still streaming out from the kitchen, and for safety's sake he stepped forward and made sure that the room was still empty.

Then he placed the box near the wall, beneath the window. It was very simple. He climbed up, testing the strength of the box gradually, without putting too much weight on it at one go. Soon he was kneeling on it, close enough to look at the frosted glass in the lower section of the window. When he stood up to his full height, he was a little too high and had to crouch down so as to peer at the window. He could see nothing, of course. Supposing he lit a match now, would there be any chance of seeing in? He tried to remember what happened if one had a small light on the outside of a window, and told himself that it was pointless; he wouldn't be able to see because the light and its reflection would dazzle him.

He had to get a light inside that shed.

So he had to break a window.

He leaned against the shed, one hand fiddling with the box of matches. They rattled reassuringly. The big box creaked, too. He reasoned consciously now, as he believed his father would. In order to look inside, he had to break a window, but there would be very little time to spare. Once he broke the window, the noise might attract people—probably including Payne. There was a risk that Payne would return to the kitchen, and he would know at once where the noise had come from; so he, Martin, had to plan this thing so that he could take a look inside the shed, check whether there was any need for alarm—check if the Yard man were a prisoner, that was the main thing—and then jump off the box and rush out so fast that he could not be stopped by anyone until he was able to summon the police. If there was no one inside that shed after all, the quicker he got away the better. No one need know who had been there, and he wouldn't make himself or his father a laughing stock.

So, the thing was to break the window, and have the light ready almost at the same time.

The best way would be to punch a hole in the window with his left hand; his thick cycling glove would give him plenty of protection, all he had to do was to make sure that he didn't cut his wrist. As he broke the glass with his left fist, he must strike a match against the wooden wall of the shed with his ungloved right hand; he could use his right hand much more dexterously, strike the match as close to the actual window as possible, then thrust the light inside. He mustn't thrust it too fast, or the wind of the movement would put it out, which would lose precious seconds. Actually, he ought to have his left hand free to shield the flame when it was first struck, so the best way would be to bend his elbow, smash the glass with that, then strike the match.

He had a kind of rehearsal. Elbow bent, cracked against the glass, remember how tough glass could be, give it a good hearty wallop. The moment it was through, strike the match with his right hand, bring his left hand back to protect the light and get a steady flame, put both hands through the broken window even at the risk of a scratch or two, and make sure that the workshop was empty.

Empty or full, he must then drop everything and run like mad towards his bicycle. He could be away in twenty seconds flat. Now that he had been over every move, and made as sure as possible that nothing could go wrong, he felt a fierce sense of excitement, and only wished that Richard were here. This was exactly the kind of daring thing Richard would revel in.

Ready?

He bent his elbow, held a match firmly, then decided that two matches held tightly together would break less easily. He took out another, placed the heads against the rough wood of the wall close to the window, and drew his left elbow back.

Go!

His elbow cracked against the glass. He felt it give. He struck the matches. *He smelt the gas*, but there was no time even for a moment of terror, because there was a blinding flash and a roar of sound, and he felt himself lifted off the box and hurled backwards.

His head cracked sickeningly against the cement of the yard, and he lay still.

The gas exploded in one blinding flash. The roar echoed about the backs of the little gardens and made many people wonder what it was. There was no fire, but inside, the gas hissed gently near Charley Fox's face.

17

WELCOME HOME

PAYNE was still in the front of the house at the time of the explosion but the windows were closed, and the sound he heard was like a car backfiring. Being at the front, the windows did not rattle, and there was nothing to suggest that anything had happened on his premises. He was in his bedroom, looking at the gas fire. In his right hand was a glass, now nearly empty of whisky and soda. He put it to his lips again, sipped, and lowered his head, staring at the fire all the time.

It was a large one.

Gwen liked warmth, that was one of the reasons for the double bed. She was a chilly mortal. She had bought that fire herself, twelve years ago, when they had first come to live here, and it had been one of her few extravagances, but neither of them had ever regretted it. It was alight now, hissing gently, so as to have the bedroom warm for the early part of the night. He could picture her standing there taking off her clothes, satiny skin gleaming in the firelight. If he were in bed, or if he were sitting and watching her, she would take every garment off slowly; the trick with the brassiere was one she used often, and it never failed to tease him. He could almost *see* her, and he would see her tonight.

Soon.

There was good time, thanks to the ape from Scotland Yard, who had said that he had to report by midnight. Gwen and the children would be home soon after ten thirty. They would be light-hearted and full of talk about the film. Maurice would start yawning first, and probably go straight to bed, and Gwen would take him a glass of warm milk in bed—or he, the father, would. In the warm milk, tonight, there would be a little sleeping draught, as there had once been in chocolates.

That was the safe course.

Hilda would go up soon after making her own milk and malt drink. As she would be more tired than usual, she would be delighted if her father took it up to her.

Then, Gwen.

Gwen always revelled in the luxury of tea in bed, and she liked her tea sweet, so there would not be the slightest reason for her to suspect that there was any drug in it. Within half an hour of the lights going out, each of them would be fast asleep, as they had been when he had gone to kill Alice Murray.

How long ago that seemed!

He had almost forgotten what Alice looked like, and had to force his mind to recall all the details of her face and her body; the pale, rather thin, flat-breasted little creature. The thought and the vision of her faded, and he saw Gwen again. He would have to be very careful tonight, because Gwen was so sensitive about his moods; he had to make sure that for at least half an hour he could behave as if he were on top of the world. It wouldn't be easy but it could be done. First, have some sandwiches and biscuits waiting for them —ah! They would want a snack tonight, he had forgotten that, so he must have sandwiches ready. They would probably have them and their drinks downstairs—and if they did it would be easier; the important thing was not to stay alone with Gwen too long, for fear she should suspect that there was something the matter.

Oh, God; Gwen!

But she mustn't know. He could not face her if she knew what he had done, what an abject failure he was. He could not face any of them again. There was no doubt that he was planning the only possible thing. He was saving them from the horror and the distress of the discovery. Unless they were dead by midnight, the police would come, and would save them.

The police would come anyhow, if the ape was right, but they would come for him, Payne. They would ask if he had seen Fox, he would deny it, and no one would have any idea what was happening upstairs. Fox would be dead by then, of course, he was probably dead now.

Was midnight long enough?

Couldn't he telephone a report to the Yard, purporting to come from Fox, saying that he had been delayed? That would hold the Yard back for a few hours, perhaps all night. There was no telling—Fox might have lied to him, and have come alone tonight, hoping to collect all the glory for himself. The wise thing was to say nothing by telephone, just wait. After all, the Yard wasn't likely to come on the stroke of twelve; if Fox reported late there would be some inquiries, probably nothing would be done for half an hour, possibly an hour or more. Even if it were, remember, all he had to say was that Fox had been to see him, and had gone away. There would be no reason for the police to come into the house or to look for Fox—they wouldn't dream of the real truth.

There was time all right, but this was the last chance.

Gwen; Maurice; Hilda.

He looked at the bedroom clock, which was on the mantelpiece over the gas fire; it was now nearly a quarter to ten. He had three quarters of an hour to get everything ready. He went out, with the fire glowing red and hissing gently. He closed the door, to make sure that the room was warm for Gwen. He went into Hilda's room, lit the gas fire there, watched it for a few seconds, and then glanced into Maurice's room; Maurice did not have the fire on often, he preferred a cold atmosphere. Payne went down on one knee and turned the tap to make sure that it was working; and such a blast of gas came that he snapped it off. He went out, and hurried downstairs. He helped himself to another whisky and soda, and then busied himself in the kitchen; only now and again did he prepare a supper snack for the family, but it had happened once or twice recently, and although they would be pleasantly surprised, there would be nothing remarkable about it.

Maurice preferred cold beef, and there was some. Gwen liked the beef with plenty of HP sauce on it; he made her sandwiches with great care, putting plenty of butter on the bread. Hilda would almost certainly rather have a cheese spread, so he made some of these, put out cheese and biscuits, then got everything ready to make the drinks. By the time he had finished it was twenty minutes past ten. Should he go and meet them? There was always the risk of missing them, and he would hate them to come home and find the house empty. On the other hand, he hadn't yet put the car away, so he had to go out for five minutes. He went to the telephone, and called the cinema.

"What time does the last performance end, please?"

"Ten thirty-five, sir, for the Queen."

"Thanks," Payne said. That gave him time to put the car away but not to go and collect the family; they wouldn't expect him, and there was a bus practically to the door. He went out the front way, and noticed a slight smell of burning, but he assumed it was from a garden fire. He walked to the car, got in, and was soon getting out again, inside the garage. He could close the main doors and go in the back way, checking on Fox as he did so, or he could go to the front. There was just a chance that the rest of the family would be early, and, in any case, he felt like going to the bus stop to meet them.

He did not want to see Fox's body. So he did not go out the back way, and therefore did not smell the gas which was escaping through the broken workshop window. He hung about the bus stop for ten minutes, then saw Gwen standing up inside a bus; he was at the stop to help her off, and he saw how pleased she was. Hilda started to talk very quickly about the feature film, holding her father's arm. Gwen walked on the other side, Maurice led the way, to open the front door. They were laughing and gay as they went inside. They would go straight into the kitchen, of course, and Gwen would want to put a kettle on right away. He went ahead, so that he could see her expression when she saw what he had prepared.

It could not have been more satisfying. Her fine eyes lit up, she beamed across at him, and Hilda, with that tendency to be over demonstrative, came across and gave him a hug. It was exactly as he had believed it would be. Maurice was looking very tired, but elected to eat downstairs and to have his milk upstairs. Hilda kept talking although her eyes looked as if they would not keep open, but she had her drink downstairs, with obvious relish.

Gwen stirred the sugar in her tea more thoroughly than usual, tucked into the sandwiches and, when the children had gone up, said :

"Are you coming to bed straight away, Jack ?"

He knew exactly what she meant. He knew that she would be asleep within half an hour, too; she was looking tired. He went across to her, took her in his arms and held her so tightly that he heard her catch her breath; then he released her, and said quietly :

"I've a bit of a headache, honey. I think I'll take a stroll after you're tucked in."

He often did that.

He heard her saying goodnight to the children; every sound and every word seemed to have a special significance. He heard her close the door of the children's rooms, and then walk across the landing to the bathroom, and, five minutes afterwards, go into their room. He went upstairs, and sat in the corner chair, by the window, watching her. She was very tired already, but nothing could alter the voluptuousness of her movements and the natural seductivenes of her body. He watched without real excitement. He saw her slide her nightdress over her head, and wriggle to make it fall down. He did not get up to go to her, but just watched. She yawned.

"I'm tired out tonight," she said. "I can't make out what's the matter with me."

"Excitement, and the thought of spending all that money, I expect!" Payne jested. He watched her get into bed, then went across and bent over her, and kissed her with a passion which seemed to well up in him, which made his heart throb and brought stinging tears to his eyes. When he drew back, he saw the way Gwen looked up at him from the pillows, and felt a sudden fear: that he had kissed her too harshly, and so warned her that something was wrong.

"You're all right, Jack, aren't you?" she asked anxiously.

"I'm fine, apart from this headache."

"If that's how a headache makes you kiss, you can have one more often," she riposted. Her eyes were bright with tiredness, and she stifled a yawn again. "Sure everything's all right?"

"It's exactly as I planned," he assured her. "I'll put out the light." In fact he knew that he was speaking with a more subdued voice than usual, that he was giving her plenty of reason for thinking that there was something the matter, but she was too tired to take much notice.

Wasn't she?

He put out the light, closed the door, and then stood listening; if she got out of bed, the springs would creak, and he would know. Had he aroused any suspicions? He heard no sound at all. He could see her in his mind's eye, lying so still. He waited for fully five minutes, then turned and went to the doors of the other rooms; there was no sound from either. He looked at his watch; it was twenty minutes past eleven. He went downstairs and poured out another whisky, without any soda this time. He sat stretched out in his arm-chair, seeing Gwen everywhere; in bed and out. He was going upstairs to lie down beside her, of course, and it was the only way. What a hell of a thing to have to do. At least he had saved them all from the knowledge which would have caused them so much hurt, it was an act he would never regret.

He gave a twisted grin; there wouldn't be much time to regret.

He waited for twenty minutes, then went upstairs. He crept into Hilda's room, and turned the gas on full, closed the door, and went into Maurice's. He had to close Maurice's window as well as draw the curtains, but the boy did not stir. When he went out, the door dragged on the carpet, so little or no gas would escape. He crossed the little landing to his own room, and went inside; he could just make out the soft sound of Gwen's breathing. He did not need a light but felt his way across to the foot of the bed, then by sense of touch to the fireplace. There was still a little warmth coming from it. He groped, found the tap, and turned it; immediately there was a loud hissing, but Gwen noticed nothing, although the escaping gas muffled the sound of her breathing. Payne eased his collar and tie, and went out. He could not be sure, but believed that an hour would be long enough; if the police did not come within the hour, he would go upstairs and lie down by Gwen's side.

Meanwhile, he had to prepare a reception party for the police, in case they came. He must be at the front of the house. He must say that Fox had been here and talked to him, and left—left only a few minutes before they had arrived. If they believed him and went off, there would be nothing to worry about. If they didn't believe him—

He knew exactly what to do.

He went into the tiny dining-room, drew the curtains, and turned on the gas fire to full strength. He went out and closed the door. If any policemen came and insisted on searching the house, he would bring them here, and as he opened the door, would flick his cigarette lighter. To make sure of getting a good flame, he refilled the lighter, and tested it several times.

A naked flame inside that room would cause a terrific explosion and send the whole house up in flames.

*   *   *

Janet West leaned forward, turned down the volume of the radio so that the music was almost inaudible, and looked across at Roger, who was buried in some Home Office crime statistics. He seemed so absorbed that she hesitated to disturb him, but when a car passed along outside, and silence followed it, she could not keep quiet any longer.

"Where *are* those boys?" she demanded.

He looked up, his eyes touched with the faraway expression which she knew only too well; give him anything to do with work, and he would lose himself in it completely

"What time is it?" He glanced at the striking clock on the mantelpiece of the front room, and raised his eyebrows. "Quarter to twelve—I suppose they are a bit late."

"They're over half an hour late," Janet said. "I never did like these eleven o'clock evenings, I don't care what you say it's too late for boys of their age to be out." Roger knew better than to grin at her. "And you can't be sure that they haven't picked up with some girls. *Richard*'s too young, even if it does amuse you that Scoopy—"

She broke off.

"I think I heard them," Roger said, and they listened intently to sounds in the street. Someone called out in a subdued voice, and Richard answered: *"Goodnight."*

"I don't hear Scoop," said Janet.

"If Richard's there, Scoop will be," Roger declared. "No, don't go and stand on the doorstep waiting for them, it's much better to let them feel grown up." When Janet sat back in her chair with a gesture of mingled exasperation and resignation, he went on: "They'll put their bikes away and be here in a couple of minutes."

He put his papers down and listened, and then began to frown.

"Roger, there *is* only one of them," Janet exclaimed, and jumped out of her chair. "Richard!" she called, knowing that the boy might hear her before he started along the passage by the side of the house. *"Richard!"* She beat Roger to the front door, and pulled it open. *"Richard!"*

Roger was just behind her.

"Hallo, Mum," Richard responded, and Roger could tell

by the tone of his voice that he wasn't as conscience-clear as he ought to be. "Isn't Scoop home yet?"

"What do you mean?" Janet demanded. "Of course he isn't home. You've been together all the evening, haven't you?"

The light fell brightly on to Richard's face. He had a slightly puffy nose, from boxing, but was not marked otherwise. There was anxiety as well as that hint of guilty conscience in his manner.

"Well, no, Mum," he confessed. "As a matter of fact, he didn't come to the club tonight. He—"

Janet went very still, but did nothing to stop the boy from telling his story. When it was half finished, Roger walked quietly to the front room, and called the Yard.

"Get in touch with Detective Sergeant Fox, find out when he last reported, see if he had anyone else working with him on the Payne investigation tonight," he ordered in short, clipped sentences. "Have a patrol car wait for me in Richmond Hill Road—get it there as soon as you can." He waited only for the response, banged down the receiver, and strode towards the door. The others were coming in, Richard looking pale and scared, and Janet saying in a tense voice:

"Roger, there's no possible danger, is there?"

"Not the slightest reason to think there is," Roger assured her. He could not tell her that Payne was suspected of two vicious murders, but there was something in his expression which warned her that he was not telling the truth. "I'm going over to the house. You wait here, and—"

"We're not waiting, we're coming," Janet declared.

*　　*　　*

The patrol car was waiting near the garden of the empty house, with some Divisional men, who had already discovered Fox's car and Martin's bicycle. There was a light on at the front of Payne's house—the only light at a window within a hundred yards.

"You watch from the other side of the road," Roger told the three men in the patrol car. "The Division will watch the back from neighbouring gardens. Jan, you and Richard must wait in the car. Don't get out—that's an order. If Payne runs for it we can't risk you getting in the way. I'll go and talk to him myself, for a start." He looked bleak and grim as he turned and went off, crossing the road and gradually looking smaller as he approached the lights at the window of Payne's house.

It was then a little after midnight.

18

LAST BLOW

ROGER saw Payne sitting in a chair near the window, craning his neck round as if he had heard footsteps and was half expecting a caller. Was he expecting the police? Roger went straight to the front door. He felt certain that Payne could not escape the cordon, and was more sure than ever that the first essential was to talk to the man. The fact that Martin had been near here for over three hours was frightening; he would have to use all the finesse he could, to make sure that no harm came to the boy—unless harm already had.

He saw Payne get up, tall, handsome, grim-faced.

Roger rang the front door bell as footsteps sounded in the passage. There was a long pause before the man drew near. Roger stood to one side, not sure what kind of reception he would get, but Payne stood outlined against the light, tall and massive in a narrow hall. Roger could just see the doorway to the right, behind the man, and the narrow staircase, which led straight to a landing which was out of sight.

"What is it?" Payne demanded gruffly.

That wasn't a normal approach, and there was nothing normal about his manner. Roger sensed his tension, and at the same time sensed danger; here was a killer, a man who might strike at any moment, savage, vicious, murderous. He wanted to see the man's face, wanted to read what he could in his eyes.

He noticed a faint—a very faint—smell of gas.

He spoke in his mildest voice, and actually managed to smile, although he was so acutely aware of Janet and Richard across the road.

"I'm sorry to worry you so late, Mr. Payne, but I wonder

184

if you can help me," he said. "I live in Bell Street—I believe you are thinking of buying a house there."

He heard Payne's heavy breathing become shallow, and was not surprised when the man drew back a little and stared, as if seeking recognition.

"I am, but I don't see how it affects you." His voice was very harsh, there was all the evidence of great tension.

"You've every right to kick me out if I'm wrong," Roger said, and smiled as if he were really sorry to be making a nuisance of himself. "Er—I have a young son, named Martin."

He could see Payne's face better, and did not think that the name of Martin meant anything to the man. He did see some indication of surprise, and thought that the physical tension in this man eased a little; that showed in the way Payne's shoulders sagged, the way his right hand dropped from the door. He was holding something in it, a petrol lighter which glinted.

"I still don't see what it's got to do with me," Payne said.

"As a matter of fact, Martin has seen your wife and daughter several times, and boy-like, he's got a crush on your daughter," Roger went on pleasantly. "Apparently he found out where you live, and came to call on her tonight. His brother says that your daughter wasn't in, and that my son Martin decided to wait. It's so late now that I wondered if you knew anything about this."

He saw Payne grin; and he sensed the man's enormous relief. He stepped forward a little, and Payne backed at once.

"Silly young pup," he said with bluff humour, "but I can't blame anyone for falling for my Hilda! She's been home and in bed the last hour, she certainly hasn't seen your kid."

"Are you quite sure?"

"Wouldn't say it if I wasn't," Payne retorted. He was obviously much more confident than he had been, and aggressiveness followed that. "The whole family was out at the pictures except me. They've been home over an hour. Your kid's probably mooning around somewhere, scared to come home."

"Possibly," said Roger, frowning. "His mother is extremely anxious about him, of course." He paused, and smelt the gas more strongly; there was much more inside the passage than there had seemed to be at the front door. The man seemed to be telling the truth, even seemed to be delighted at the turn of events, but he wouldn't be delighted for long. He went on, without changing his tone of voice: "Where is my man Fox, Mr. Payne?"

He saw Payne's mouth tighten, saw his eyes narrow, saw how his body seemed to gather itself for some physical effort. A car horn tooted lightly, from across the road; that would be Janet. She would be able to see Roger so far, but when he went further into the house and was out of sight, she would probably find it impossible to stay in the car.

"I don't know what the hell you're talking about," Payne growled.

"I think you do," Roger said. "He was coming to ask you some questions tonight—about the murder of Jennie Campbell. I am a police officer, and—"

"Damned swine!" Payne's lips hardly seemed to open as he spoke, and he must have realised that the change in his manner had given him away. He put his left hand to his lips, and raised the cigarette lighter a little; it was a very large one. "I haven't seen anyone except my family tonight, and I don't know any Jennie Campbell."

Roger said: "Payne, that kind of lie won't help you. A hundred people can prove that you knew Jennie." He was close enough now to make quite sure that there was no physical danger from the other, and yet could not quite understand the situation or Payne's attitude. Martin might not have been inside here, but Fox probably had, remember.

There was that smell of gas.

"So you're calling me a liar," Payne growled, and then changed his tactics, and went on in a jeering way: "So I'm a liar. What difference does it make?" He backed away again, and was obviously doing that deliberately, wanting to draw Roger on. *Why?* "All right, Fox came to see me tonight, and we had a little argument," Payne admitted savagely. "He said that someone else would come after him and I thought he was lying—but he wasn't. Proper little George Washington, isn't he?" Payne threw back his head and laughed; there was something wild and uncontrolled in the harsh sound which came out. He backed further away. "He's waiting in here, hoping that you'll come for him," he growled. "I've got enough sense to know when I'm beaten, blast you."

He put his right hand to the door.

He moved his left hand, with the lighter, in front of him, yet there was no obvious reason for it, Roger thought desperately. There was no obvious reason and yet there must be a reason.

Gas!

Payne was turning the handle.

Roger didn't speak, didn't waste a second, just slammed his clenched fist to the small of Payne's back. As the man staggered, Roger snatched at the lighter, and clutched it. Payne kicked out at him and tried to get it back, but he had lost his balance. The door was unfastened and his waving hand banged against it, and it swung open.

A billow of gas swept out.

Roger thought, with strange calmness: *I hope to God Scoop's all right*, and hooked Payne's legs from under him. As the man pitched forward into the gas-filled room, Roger bellowed:

"*Help, there! Hurry!*" He heard footsteps on the instant; men would be here within thirty seconds, and there was nothing more he could do. The stench of gas made him feel sick, and he retched. He saw Payne scrambling to his feet, but men were already at the front porch. He went forward and grabbed Payne's right wrist, twisted it roughly and made the man cry out, pushed him round so that he could thrust the right arm up behind him in a hammer-lock.

"Where's my son?" he demanded savagely. "And where's Fox. Come on, Payne—"

Then he heard an exclamation from behind him. He heard Janet cry out, her voice so clear that it seemed to strike horror into him; the cry itself was filled with horror.

"*Scoop!*" she cried, as if in awful despair. "*Scoop!*"

Roger thrust Payne away from him, pushed past two of the men from the Squad car, heard voices outside, heard Janet screaming again, heard Richard cry out as if he were trying to restrain his mother, and then saw his elder son staggering from the passage between the house and the garage, blackened and burned, his hair just a frizzy black mess, his eyes looking wild as a madman's. He saw Scoopy's lips moving, knew that he was trying to offer some reassurance. Richard was gripping his hands tightly and holding his head high, chin thrust forward, as if in some kind of frenzy. Then Roger reached Janet and Scoopy at the same time, took Janet's arm and said urgently:

"He's all right, Janet, he's all right."

But he was terribly afraid.

*　　*　　*

"He's all right," the police surgeon said, straightening up from the grass plot where Scoopy had been put down, at full length. "He'll be without much hair for a few weeks, and he's got a few first degree burns, but it looks as if his gloved left hand took most of the flames, and saved his face and his eyes. He's all right, Mrs. West."

Janet didn't speak.

Richard was staring across the road, at the dozens of people gathering now, at the police cars and the ambulance which had been sent for immediately, and at two ambulance men who were coming for Scoopy.

Roger said: "He'll be all right, Jan. Take it easy."

He knew that a great deal was happening both inside the

house and outside. Men from the Division had arrived and gone through the house, and Scoopy had tried to tell them about a shed at the back. More men had gone hurrying there, but Roger did not know exactly what had happened. But his son was not badly hurt, and nothing else seemed to matter. That, and getting Janet away from here. He should have known that directly the worst of the shock was past, Janet would have only one purpose: to go in the ambulance to the hospital. That was the best thing for her, too, as well as for Richard. It would allow time for him to sort things out here, and then go and fetch them.

Janet said, as if she expected a lot of opposition: "I don't care what you say, I'm going with my son."

"Fish, go with them and look after them, won't you?" Roger said.

When the ambulance had driven off, a Divisional man came up and said, briskly, that another ambulance would be needed. Fox had been found, with severe wounds at the back of his head, some burns, and in an advanced state of carbon monoxide poisoning. There was the smell of gas everywhere, the ringing of ambulance bells, the roar of engines. Then another man thrust his way forward from the house, and said:

"It's one of the worst things I've ever come up against, Mr. West. Payne's wife and two children are unconscious upstairs, he turned the gas full on in their rooms. God knows whether they'll survive or not. I've sent for another ambulance."

Roger said: "Oh, God, what a mess." He moved forward, saying: "I'll go and look." He coughed as he entered the house, which was still reeking with gas, and called back: "Go and make sure no one's smoking and that there's no naked light within fifty yards, even out in the street." A man answered: "Right, sir!" Roger went up the little staircase, with its half landing, its cheap banisters, its vivid red wall-paper. He saw all the three bedroom doors wide open, and felt a wind coming in from the front and blowing right through. He went into the bathroom, which was hardly large enough to turn round in, soaked a towel and put it round his face, then went into the first of the three rooms— the largest. Payne's wife lay on her back, her face a bright cherry pink, her arms and shoulders the same hideous colour. Roger felt quite sure that she was dead; the only possible hope would be hospital treatment.

Roger went to see the girl, who looked more naturally asleep. A man by a window said :

"There's a good vent by the side of the chimney in this room, I should think a lot of gas went up that way. She ought to be all right."

"Good," Roger said. He stared at the girl, and understood what his son saw in her, and wondered what the future held. Then he went to see Payne's boy, who was quite as far gone as his mother.

"Almost makes you hope the girl will go, too, doesn't it?" the Yard man said.

Payne was standing in the hall, handcuffed to a Divisional man who had made the charge. From here, he appeared to have lost every vestige of colour. His shoulders were bowed, and he leaned against the wall in an attitude of absolute dejection. When a man told him to move, he did not really straighten up, but seemed to drag himself towards the front door. When he reached it, he turned to look round, and to look upwards; Roger had never seen such despair on a human face.

Roger heard him ask : "They will die, won't they? They won't live to know what happened."

"You can do your talking later," the detective said roughly, and obviously tugged at Payne, who went out and disappeared.

Soon, doctors, ambulance men and men from the Gas Board were crowding the little house, and Roger went downstairs. A radio report from the hospital said that Fox would pull through; no one then knew that he would owe his life to the broken window. The news about Scoopy was about the same, but his single head wound was much less serious than Fox's.

"No reason why you shouldn't leave the clearing up to us, Handsome," a Divisional man said. "You'll want to see your son. Why don't you call it a day? We've got Payne as tight as a drum, the devil. He'll hang."

And his daughter would probably live.

Roger went to the hospital, only ten minutes' drive away, and found Janet normal except for tear-stained face and smeared lipstick, and Richard talking much more than usual, his tired eyes very bright as he explained again exactly what had happened. Scoopy was under a sleeping drug.

"But there's nothing at all to worry about," Janet said. "He'll be all right, thank God, he'll be all right."

She didn't know, nobody knew, just how close Roger had been to being blown to death before his son had recovered consciousness, and staggered round to the front of the house.

*   *   *

Next morning, Roger went to see Julian Anderson. There was a special court arranged for that afternoon, when the police would formally submit that they had no evidence, and the charges would be withdrawn.

It was the first time he had seen Julian's slow smile.

*   *   *

Three months later, Payne was hanged.

His daughter, who was staying with relatives, had been in court throughout the trial. She had lost her colouring and her vitality, and seemed very much thinner and older than when she had first come to Bell Street. Scoopy saw her in court twice, but she showed no interest in him, and they did not speak. Fox had recovered sufficiently to give evidence about the steel filings and the fingerprints on the chocolate boxes found in Alice Murray's room, which were identical with Payne's.

After the execution, Roger learned, Hilda planned to

emigrate to one of the Dominions; her mother had left her a little money, and there was some to come from her father's estate.

On the day after the execution, two middle-aged and rather aloof looking people moved into Cornerways. Very little had been said about the house by any of the West family, but it was tacitly accepted that it was not the right home for them.

Soon after Hilda left the country, Julian Anderson called at the house in Bell Street, spruce, immaculate, almost himself again, yet still not a man to like. He had with him a set of Georgian jewellery, not expensive but very lovely, and he stood with his back to the window in the shabby front room, and said:

"I know one cannot make a gift to a police officer, Mr. West, and I would not like to cause any embarrassment for you, but I must somehow show my appreciation of the way you treated me during those terrible days. So I bring this gift to your charming wife. I always felt that you would exert yourself to the uttermost to see that justice was done. That is a very reassuring feeling, Mr. West, very reassuring indeed."

He held out his flabby hand.

Martin called Scoopy and Richard saw him leave and wanted to know who he was. Martin showed no signs of the burns or the injuries, and Richard seemed to have grown a couple of inches in the past few months. To Janet, in a queer way they seemed to have grown younger, too.

Date D